IMMORTAL FLAME

Hell to Pay: Book 1

JILLIAN DAVID

Crimson Romance
New York London Toronto Sydney New Delhi

CRIMSON
ROMANCE

Crimson Romance
An Imprint of Simon & Schuster, Inc.
1230 Avenue of the Americas
New York, NY 10020

CRIMSON ROMANCE and colophon are trademarks of Simon & Schuster, Inc.

ISBN 978-1-4405-8914-0
ISBN 978-1-4405-8915-7 (ebook)

Acknowledgments

Big thanks to my husband, who kept asking, "When will you stop writing and just go sell that book?" He also posed very helpful advice such as, "Make sure your hero is bald. And short. We need representation, too."

I would never be writing this acknowledgement page without having met editor extraordinaire, Gwen Hayes. She simply edited and taught. And she did so with kindness and a great sense of humor.

Thanks also to other key editors along the way: Bev Rosenbaum, Devin Govaere, and Annie Seaton with her secret editing associate. I am reluctant to list these folks here only because I'm revealing my secret weapons.

Finally, thanks to editor Julie Sturgeon and the fine team at Crimson. You all have taken a story I'm proud of and elevated it to a new level. Thank you for the patience and suggestions.

Chapter 1

Old things weren't always useless. Take the Swiss watch Peter Blackstone wore. Tired leather strap, scratched face, older than most mortals. He had taken it off the wrist of an enemy, a dying *Wehrmacht* captain, in the icy forest of northern France in retaliation for the captain shooting Peter in the arm. Call it a souvenir turned taunting, old, reliable companion.

Not that the damned watch helped the traffic. A cold mist slowed the cars on I-84 outside La Grande, Oregon. Steep, pine-rich mountains rose on either side, funneling bumper-to-bumper vehicles into the narrow canyon. No gritting of Peter's teeth or clenching of the steering wheel could stop that interminable timepiece from tick, tick, ticking down like a demolition bomb timer, reminding him how late he would be and the likely outcome of his tardiness.

His final assignment. He hoped.

Damn endless existence. He needed to complete this last assignment, the Meaningful Kill. Finally put an end to the monster he'd become.

His gut knotted. Being late for his assignment created too much attention. Better to stay inconspicuous. Hell, he wore a seat belt only so police wouldn't have a reason to ticket him. Too much to explain.

The semi ten inches from his front bumper flashed its brakes. Peter slowed and negotiated one of the curves on the stretch of road. He rubbed his jaw and glanced again at the watch.

Hell, even now, he could smell the sweet-sharp scent of snow and blood and hear the moans from the not-yet-dead as bodies littered the forest that ugly night in the Ardennes. Men crying out for their mothers in English and German, the sounds blending into a nightmare of suffering, as they were frozen alive.

He glanced in the rearview mirror out of habit. Even after all these years, his dark brown hair would never turn gray, no matter how much he wished to age. It was the curse of the Indebted.

Screeching tires jolted him back to reality. *Hell.* He swerved and barely missed the braking semi. The driver behind him wasn't as quick, and the pickup plowed into the back of Peter's SUV, propelling it into the concrete barrier. Air whooshed out of his lungs as he jerked against the seat belt. His neck snapped forward as a ripping sensation seared pain into the base of his skull.

His SUV ramped the barrier, the undercarriage screaming against wet concrete. Peter's entire world inverted, sky beneath him and rocks above, with only a thin casing of metal standing between his head and the scraping rocks. *Not good.* He threw his hands over his head and pushed against the charcoal upholstery in time for the airbag to erupt from the steering wheel. His ribcage exploded in sharp, hot agony that sent fireworks of light bursting in his vision.

After that, it was as if his own car waged a personal assault on him. But the blade would be no match against the airborne missiles of glass piercing his face. To make things even more interesting, the SUV righted itself but then jolted halfway down the mountain slope.

Peter's head snapped forward and back, and a loud crack reverberated from his lower back, out of tune with the groans and screeches emanating from the nearly obliterated vehicle.

An eternity later—he didn't use the term lightly—the crumpled metal death trap came to rest at the bottom of a muddy embankment, the yellow hazard lights flashing, horn blaring … and upside down.

Stunned, Peter dangled from the seat belt. His ears rang. His skull throbbed. His left arm had bent into an unnatural angle against the door handle. *Not good at all.* A normal human would be dead by now. Unfortunately, he still lived.

Hell. He was most definitely going to be late for that appointment.

The knife strapped to his lower leg pulsed, warming up in hungry anticipation for the assignment. That damned, cursed weapon tied to his damned, cursed existence.

The sky and ground continued to spin in his vision. Over the hum of his ringing ears, liquid drizzled onto the fabric ceiling, a constant tapping sound in the sudden silence. One touch to his head revealed a chunk of skin partially detached from his skull.

Steam hissed from the engine as the tangy-sweet scent of antifreeze mixed with burnt oil. Taking a deep breath, he dragged fumes into his burning lungs. From far away, voices drifted down to him.

Pain lanced through his neck when he tried to see out the window. He had to fix that broken arm.

Damn, this is going to hurt.

With his right hand, he grabbed his left wrist and pulled. His guttural howl echoed in the destroyed car as he forced arm bones back into place, grinding the broken ends against each other. He squeezed his hand over the injury. The arm had started to knit, but he needed the bones to heal even faster. His body would repair the life-threatening injuries first and his head and broken bones second, but it would take way too much time.

The whine of his car's smoking engine and drone of the horn muffled the shouts of bystanders scrambling down the hill.

Have to get out of here.

He attempted to exit the car, leaning against the mangled door, but his numb legs wouldn't move. They'd lodged between the pedals pushed in by the crumpled engine block and the steering column. Instinctive fear rose up. Trapped again. He forced himself to relax while suspended upside down. In the distance sirens wailed.

So much for being inconspicuous.

Damn it. He needed to stash the knife before anyone saw it.

Reaching his unbroken arm down—no, up—to the pinned, insensate leg, Peter unclasped the top strap of the holster. One more strap. As he strained against the seat belt, pain erupted in his lower back, but now he could touch the lower clasp.

The voices of his rescuers drew closer, urging him to work faster. Frantic, he brushed the buckle with this fingertips and opened the clasp. Fresh sweat beaded his brow, and his jaw ached from clenching.

The strap slid free of the buckle, and the knife fell to the roof with a dull *thunk*, landing in pooled blood. The physical agony of separation from the weapon hit him like a punch to his gut. The yearning to connect with the blade burned with a searing inferno in his chest.

Focus.

Stretching, he grabbed the knife and shoved it into the seam of the passenger seat.

He gritted his teeth as another wave of pain swamped him.

• • •

It had been one month and twelve days since her last vision.

Allison La Croix pulled her hair from the jacket collar, straightened her scrubs, and closed the car door. Hefting her overnight bag onto her shoulder, she paused and inhaled the cold, early spring air. Could she do it today? Could she walk through the doors of Grande Ronde Hospital's emergency department?

Every day when she passed through those sliding glass doors, apprehension mounted like a needle tip poised just above her skin. Her right hand still throbbed with residual echoes of electrical fire on her fingertips from her last connection. How long could she avoid touching anyone skin to skin? How long could she avoid triggering her twisted gift? The intervals between her visions were growing shorter, but she had no idea why. How many more could she handle?

With a determined breath, she entered the ER at 7:55 a.m., right on time. Ambulance bays vacant? Check. No screaming family members outside the ER door? Check. No *whump, whump* of chopper blades coming in for a landing? Double check.

Maybe today will be a good day.

She twisted her long hair into a clip as the familiar flowery scent of chemical disinfectant wafted over her. As Allison reached the registration desk, she waved at a plump, smiling, older woman.

"Morning, Doctor Al," the woman said.

"Hi, Marcie. How's it been so far?"

The receptionist held up the latest bestselling medical thriller. "Real calm. I've had time to catch up on some reading."

Allison smiled at her choice of words. Doctors and staff *never* said the "Q" word when they came onto shift. Merely thinking the word "quiet" seemed to magically attract multi-victim traumas, drug-seekers, and large quantities of cardiac arrests.

"You think it's going to rain today?" Allison asked.

She averted her gaze as Marcie changed the computer screen from a shopping website to the hospital registration system.

"Hope so. Maybe light rain later. The Wallowas look good. Might get more snow next weekend."

To the east, powdery snow covered the 9,000-foot peaks of the Wallowa Mountains. She'd give anything to be up there right now, surrounded by the mellow scent of pine, serenaded by the burble of clear water running down the valleys. Hiking or snowshoeing, it didn't matter; either was like aloe on a burn to Allison's soul.

Walking to the back of the ER, she dropped her overnight bag on an empty chair in the doctor's work area. She waited until her graying counterpart, Dr. Buddy Clark, finished a dictation, his voice gravelly. His shoulders sagged from the twenty-four-hour shift, which had also deepened the circles beneath his kind eyes.

She thanked her thirty-two-year-old body for its youth; at least she recovered much faster than her sixty-something colleague.

"Anything I can take care of for you?" she asked.

"Not this morning. Last night was pretty tame, long may it last." He made the sign of a cross, merrily kissed his fingers, and raised them as his eyes twinkled. Buddy, cheerful even when tired, was nothing if not consistent with his superstitions.

"Don't jinx me." She patted him on the back, careful not to touch his skin.

"Hey, Al, did you consider my offer to set you up with that physical therapist?" He leaned back in his chair and rubbed his stubbled jowls. "He'd be a perfect match. Educated, outdoorsy, probably a good family guy. Cute, but not too metrosexual. Ruggedly handsome."

She cringed. A family guy? God, no. Too many risks. The possibility of another vision of a loved one filled her with cold terror. She couldn't trust herself to invest in a relationship when all she would think about was when that next vision of death would arrive. No, thank you. She wasn't putting herself through that pain ever again.

At least working in the hospital allowed some semblance of purpose, an opportunity to perform penance. Here she could make a difference, atone for the devastating knowledge her ability yielded. If she had the power to randomly see the death of people she touched, at least the medical training gave her the ability to save other peoples' lives. Saving someone—anyone—made up for the inevitable deaths she predicted. Her gift might have been easier to manage if she got images when she touched every person, or if she knew which people would trigger her visions, but no, she received sudden, random pain instead. The nasty surprises never got easier, even after years of avoiding hugs, declining to brush her niece's hair, and refusing to kiss her own sister's cheek at her wedding. Allison only risked direct touch when she had no other choice. She only risked touch when she felt emotionally braced, and that wasn't often.

"Aw, thanks for thinking of me, Buddy, but I've got enough on my plate right now. Why don't you get on home? Enjoy your day off."

• • •

A few hours later, an ambulance pulled up to the entrance of the Grande Ronde ER, lights flashing and sirens blaring. Allison raced out of the warm ER into the crisp air, her body heated by zips of adrenaline. Already gloved up, she met the patient as the EMTs called for help to unload his gurney from the ambulance. The patient moaned and strained against the backboard straps, then lapsed into unconsciousness. Her five-second assessment as they rolled him into the ER was grim: facial trauma, bleeding flap of scalp that was thankfully still attached, loss of consciousness.

"Are there more victims?" she asked an EMT.

The EMT maneuvered the gurney into the small trauma room. "No, just this lucky guy. His car launched over the interstate barrier and down the embankment. He almost went into the creek."

She breathed a sigh of relief. At least she could focus on one patient. "Do we know anything about this guy? Name? Age? Any medical problems?"

The EMT shrugged. "State troopers told us to get him to the hospital and they'd look for ID later."

Then she'd have to work blind. "Let's get a cross-table C-spine stat. And a trauma panel."

Nurses and EMTs carefully transferred the patient, who lay still and silent, secured on the backboard, to the ER bed. The staff unstrapped the man and quickly cut away his bloodstained T-shirt and faded jeans. An empty knife holster on his lower leg gave her pause, but her curiosity disappeared with the rest of his clothing.

At last, they had him draped in a hospital gown and covered with a starched hospital sheet.

Allison placed the bell of her stethoscope over the man's broad chest. Normal heart rate. Lungs clear. Pressing on his ribcage dusted with dark hair and his flat abdomen, she found no crepitus or rigidity. She inhaled deeply.

A nurse raised an eyebrow. "Anything?"

"No trace of alcohol or drugs." All she smelled was the metallic scent of blood and a typical male essence like almonds and very faint cologne.

With the Velcro straps off, the staff carefully logrolled him to one side, a maneuver that kept his neck, spine, and hips in safe alignment so she could evaluate his back for injuries. Once the staff rolled him back onto the backboard and re-secured the wide straps, radiology personnel shot a quick neck x-ray.

A final assessment of his muscled extremities completed the exam. She felt oddly flushed, like his skin radiated too much heat. Strange.

When she touched him, a vibration flowed through her gloved hands. She had never gotten a vision through gloves. Then again, she'd never gotten a warning signal, either. What the hell was going on here? The vibration jolted up her arms.

Oh God, not now. Please wait until I finish treating this man. Please.

"Do we have a set of vitals?" she asked.

Her patient breathed on his own, unlabored. An old, scratched watch with a dried leather band was fastened around his thick, tanned wrist. Despite the horrific bruises over his body, only his head injury needed intervention. Damn it, she had to examine his wound. She shook her hand, hesitated, then took a deep breath and braced herself. When she lifted the palm-sized flap of scalp, it bled into his dark hair until she taped the gauze back down. She could repair the wound after the CT scan. Jerking her hand away from the buzzing sensation, she pulled off her gloves and replaced them with a clean pair.

She stepped away from her patient and relaxed. Maybe this man's injuries weren't as life threatening as she had initially thought.

The EMT frowned. "Blood pressure is one thirty over ninety, pulse eighty, respiration sixteen, temperature … 107?"

"Okay." She stared at the EMT. "Wait. What? Could you retake that temperature, please? That can't be right."

"Ma'am, I already rechecked it with a different machine. It's 107.3 to be exact."

With her heart thudding, she searched the unconscious man for obvious signs of infection or malignant hyperthermia from drug use, anything to explain the temperature reading.

"Start him on IV fluids and get a cooling blanket hooked up."

Screw those visions, she had to touch him again. She needed to figure out what was wrong with this patient before his brain fried.

She eased his eyes open and flashed her penlight. Normal pupillary responses. The deep brown, almost black color of his eyes surprised her with their darkness. His open eye locked onto hers and focused, at the same time a blast of vibration drilled from his face through her hand.

The depth of that gaze pulled her like a particle into a black hole. Her heart expanded then contracted, and her breath caught. Vertigo washed over her. She grabbed the IV pole for balance. The rush of vision took hold, blocking out all sound, like voices obscured by a stiff wind. Faces swam too quickly to make out details. Far in the distance of her mind's eye, the focus sharpened onto a man. She could see—

A radiology tech tapped her on the arm. "Doc? Doc?"

Allison moved her hand away. The patient's eye fell closed, and the vortex sensation ebbed.

For the space of two breaths, she felt like a woman surfacing from under water. "Yes?"

"C-spine x-ray is here for your review, and CT is warmed up and ready if this guy's okay to go." The tech passed her a plastic film.

The nurses turned on the water-cooling blanket now draped over the man. Allison could run him through the scanner with the blanket on top of him. But damn it, why was his temperature so high? Broken neck? Head injury?

She lifted the film to the light. No obvious vertebral fracture, so it was safe to move the patient. "Sure thing. I'll go with you."

Once they arrived in the CT room, the staff transferred the man's backboard into the scanner, handling the man with ease, though to look at him, he must have been 200 pounds of solid muscle. This guy gave Captain America a run for his money.

The machine whirred and hummed. Images of his head, thorax, and abdomen slowly downloaded onto the computer screen. Allison leaned forward. No obvious internal bleeding or spinal injuries. No chest or abdomen damage. The overview scan revealed callus formation on his skull, forearm, and ribs, no doubt from old, healed fractures. A few minutes later, the standard scan images appeared. Where she'd noted callus formations before, now there were none. These new scans belonged to a man with no previous fractures. But how?

She glanced between the crash victim and his inconsistent scans. How did a man crash at fifty-five miles per hour and destroy his vehicle without so much as a hairline fracture? And what would explain the hyperthermia?

Allison rubbed her tight neck muscles. "What do you think? I'm not a radiologist, but it looks good to me."

The tech gave the okay sign and put a finger to his lips. "I'll have the radiologist call in a few minutes with the official word. This guy was lucky."

"Yeah, lucky." She stared at the screen and then back to the enigma on the other side of the lead glass window.

When the staff moved him back to the trauma room, his feet hung over the end of the gurney. He had to be well over six feet tall, maybe mid-thirties, probably a healthy guy. So why the temperature? Why the ghosts on the CT scan?

She reviewed the labs. White cell count was normal. Okay, so no infection. Drug screen negative. And the CT was negative, so the hyperthermia wasn't due to brain damage. Her pulse sped up as she called for the nurse to start cooled IV fluids. She had to try something to help this man, but damned if she knew what the hell she was treating. Shivers skittered up and down her neck, part frustration and part fear for this man's life.

When things don't add up in the ER, people end up dead.

Marcie poked her head into the doctor's work area. "Teleradiology's on the phone." Allison picked up the line, ready for her colleague to shed light on the mystery of this patient.

"Hi, Al, it's Becca Lawson in Baker City."

"What do you see?"

"Nothing much. What was the mechanism of injury?"

"Car went down the bank off the interstate, rolled a couple times. Restrained passenger, stable in the ER, with a head lac that I'll sew up in a few." She paused. "Oh, and a temperature reading of 107. I can't find any reason for that. He should at least be sweating and seizing by now, with markers of muscle breakdown. Yet there's nothing on lab. You see anything to explain it on your side?"

"No, his head is fine. There's some swelling near the head wound and some facial bruises. I presume he's black and blue?"

"Uh-huh."

"His neck and spine are clear, no swelling, no fracture. Abdomen and chest are clear." She whistled low. "Are you sure you've got the right patient? I'd say this guy cheated death."

"It's the right guy. Anything to explain the hyperthermia? Maybe something in the midbrain?"

14

"Hmm." Taps and mouse clicks transmitted through the phone. "Nothing. No blood, no swelling. Did you check your thermometer?"

Allison blew an exasperated breath. "Yes, it's reading correctly."

"Don't know." Dr. Lawson chuckled. "This is why I have the computer screen and not a stethoscope."

"Ugh. Thanks, Becca." She set down the phone and pressed her fingers to the bridge of her nose.

A nurse's scream shattered the silence.

Chapter 2

"Stop it!" Allison stepped into the fray. "Stop it!" she shouted at the man.

He froze.

Her patient, fully awake now, had *sat up* while still attached to the backboard—now in two pieces. She'd never seen anyone break a board before. She hadn't even thought such an act was humanly possible. The Velcro straps should have torn first.

Nurses hung on as the man struggled to free his arms, his muscles bulging. One IV line had ripped out. Dark blood dripped from his arm to the floor until a nurse pressed four-by-four gauze pads onto the IV site.

"Get. Me. Out. Of. Here," he ground out, his strong jaw immobilized by the cervical collar.

"Okay, cool it."

He followed her every move with a dark brown gaze fixed on her.

She gulped. "First of all, your CT scan is clear. So if you calm down for a second, we can get you out of the collar and off of what's left of our backboard."

He tensed briefly and then relaxed as the nurses took the collar and backboard on their way out the door. When he swung both legs around to the side of the bed, his feet touched the floor. He stared at Allison to the point where heat crawled up her neck onto her face. Even covered in blood, bandaged up, and bruised, this handsome man oozed intensity. A flutter in her belly reminded her to stay professional.

"Okay, Mister … ?"

He paused, brows furrowed for a long moment, then met her gaze with an astonished expression. His handsome face lit up as if he remembered something important.

Her mouth went dry.

"Blackstone. Peter Blackstone." His rumbling, low voice ran right though her, and Allison suppressed the urge to shiver.

"All right, Mr. Blackstone, since you're awake, let me ask you a few questions—"

With a slash of his hand, he cut her off. "I need *you* to answer some questions. Where am I? What happened? Who are you? What did I say to you people earlier?" He rubbed his hand over the knot on his forehead.

She took a deep breath. "Okay, then. You're in La Grande, Oregon. The EMTs extracted you from your SUV, which rolled down an embankment. You and your demolished vehicle almost ended up in the river. You haven't said a word since you got here, on account of being unconscious. And I'd say you're pretty lucky you can move *and* talk after that bad of an accident. As for who I am? I'm Dr. La Croix, the doctor who is trying to help you." *Some thanks.*

She turned toward the counter and snapped on a pair of gloves. When she glanced over her shoulder, the stark, lost expression on his hard features made her pause. Her tone softened. "Now, I'd like to keep patching you back together. So if you don't mind, I need to take care of that cut on your head. Would you please lie back?"

He stared at her.

Her pulse pounded in her ears.

Finally, he complied, scowling at her until the hairs rose on her arms. His eyebrows quirked as if he wanted to ask a question. Tension radiated from bunched muscles as he lay stiffly, his substantial frame nearly covering the entire bed. While she unwrapped the bandages and examined his scalp, he stared at the ceiling. A nurse returned and held up the Xylocaine so Allison could draw it up into a syringe.

After she irrigated the wound, the flap wasn't bleeding as much as when he'd first entered the ER. Actually, most of the area that had been pouring out blood earlier had healed, leaving a simple laceration to repair. *Bizarre.* Scalp wounds often appeared worse than they actually were. Maybe that was the case here.

When she injected the Xylocaine, she had to double check that Peter was conscious, because he didn't flinch when she inserted the needle. She brought the skin edges together, the squeak and click of the skin stapler uncomfortably loud in the trauma bay. Heat poured off his skin, and that strange vibration traveled through her gloves. Although she surreptitiously shook her hand out and used instruments to manipulate his wound edges, the vibration continued, like her hand hovered a millimeter above a high-voltage power line.

Damn it. Not again.

She threw the gloves into the trash and rubbed her hands on her scrub pants, praying her fingertips would stop buzzing. She scooted the stool around to the side of the bed while a nurse removed the laceration repair tray.

"All done," Allison said.

Peter sat on the side of the bed, the hospital gown covering most of his thighs. His large hands rested on his knees above long, muscular lower legs dusted with dark hair. His corded forearms flexed as he leaned forward.

Her heart skipped a beat when he locked those dark eyes onto her.

With the room now empty of staff, the silence crackled like someone had flipped a switch to that same high-voltage power line. She cleared her throat to talk, but he interrupted her.

"Can I leave now?"

She sputtered. "Excuse me? No, you have a head injury."

He snorted.

"You need to stay overnight for observation."

"Not going to happen." He stood, towering over her.

She instinctively reached out to steady her patient.

Electric fire coursed through her hand where she touched Peter's naked forearm. Her hand ached, burned, and froze all at the same time. Terrible pain smothered her in an unending, red-hot haze.

Her gift—randomly seeing the death of the person she touched—went haywire. She'd never seen annihilation of human beings like this before. Too much, too quickly. She couldn't filter the images, couldn't control the rate of input into her mind.

Images jammed into her head. Blazing agony was the frame upon which this vision took shape. Blurs of activity and roars of sound coalesced into specific people and objects. Fields were littered with bodies ... soldiers? But the uniforms weren't right. It looked like an army hospital, but the equipment seemed older, much older. In a blink, there was a flash of light and a scalding ache in her arm.

Then the image shifted to a woman's face ... her sweet smile ... then she shriveled into herself and became a living skeleton with eyes sunken deep into her face. The woman's pitiful sobs hit Allison like a punch to the abdomen. Then a man appeared, his features obscured in dark smoke except for a malicious smirk. Instinctively, Allison recoiled from the waves of evil emanating from the man. How did she know that he was evil? She mentally shrugged. In whatever manner she experienced this vision, she simply knew for a fact—could feel—that this man promised nothing but horror to anyone around him.

A familiar large, tanned hand reached out as if it came from within her body and shook the evil man's smoking hand. Relief washed over Allison, along with hope ...

Then a terrible realization.

Horror iced her veins and settled like a frozen fist clenched inside her chest. By some twist of her already warped powers, she had moved inside Peter's mind. The only question: did these visions represent his imagination or real experiences?

Unable to control the visions, her mind's eye was forced in a different direction. She saw the skeletal woman again, this time her round face full of life, with a doting young man by her side and a baby on her hip. Bittersweet happiness turned to pain as it lanced through Allison's chest and then the image disappeared, only to be replaced by more visions.

Piercing screams, hands reaching for her but only grasping air, bulging eyes staring at the end of their lives, painful gasps—her vision presented a parade of horror that had no end.

For what felt like an eternity, she simply watched people die. Asian men in green uniforms, then dark-haired, olive-skinned men. People died from the hands that seemed to be a part of her. Blood spurted from knife wounds coming from one specific weapon, a blade about a foot long and glowing green. People collapsed as the tanned hands released from around reddened necks. In her vision, she heard reports of gunfire, but always the vision returned to the eerie knife.

Another jolt of power and hope washed over her, followed by crushing, deep despair. After the hands let go of a neck, the knife plunged into a body. Again, she felt a burst of hope and then despair.

This connection with the visions had never happened before. She had no idea why, but the texture of her usual visions had changed in such a way that she was actually experiencing killing people. Never before had she been the cause of the pain. Never had she felt her own hand push a weapon and rend bone and flesh.

So much death, so much suffering—like a superheated vase in a kiln, Allison's soul began to crack. Trapped in the vision, she couldn't breathe, couldn't call for help. The pressure in her mind threatened to tear her apart. She'd seen death before, but never in this vicious way. Never this real, this immediate. Never was she the killer.

Suddenly, she was lying on the hospital bed. Peter's black stare filled her sight.

• • •

Peter's life seemed to stop and start the instant the gentle doctor touched his arm. The emotions reflected in her lovely emerald eyes shifted from concern to unrelenting agony as her pale lips pressed together and blood drained from her face. Physically connected as they were, he caused her suffering, and he hated himself for it. But, oh, he did love that rush of raw power that flowed from her hand into his body. He'd never felt anything like that electric power before. Did the voltage surge have to do with this woman, or had his inhuman state suddenly changed? The flow of power had to be from the woman now curled on the floor.

According to his blasted, ever ticking watch, the experience had lasted mere seconds in real time, but to him it was an eternity of blissful freedom.

Somehow, her contact had lifted the weight from his long-suffering soul. Everything was gone: the guilt after each kill, the disappointment that he would have to continue killing, the pain from his ultimate sacrifice too many years ago. The succor was like sunlight and fresh air in his stale lungs. Standing this close, she even smelled of a bright, sunny day or a clear mountain stream. And he craved more. He craved her.

They'd connected in a way he'd never known with another person, human or otherwise. He thought he'd left the balm of human touch behind many decades ago.

He had been wrong.

Maybe there was some humanity left. Then again, maybe not, since he also wanted to feel this way forever, despite what it would do to this woman. A shocking, delectable mixture of raw power and protectiveness washed over him.

He no longer wanted to leave the hospital.

Peter wanted more.

More of this energy, this control.

More of her.

But now, with their connection broken, his soul grew dark and empty, as though his loss from years ago had happened once again.

Careful not to touch her skin, he slid his hands below her shoulders and knees. When he brushed his lips over the strands of silky hair that had come loose from the clip, he inhaled her scent of fresh air and flowers. Her delicate frame fit next to him like a puzzle piece.

A puzzle piece he didn't want to let go.

When she moaned, he willed himself to relax his tight grip.

He could kill any human with his bare hands, and on one level, that ability had served him well. On the other hand, that power reminded him of the creature he had become and the terror he'd been forced to deliver. His unnatural strength was a side effect of the price he had paid to save someone he loved.

He gently laid her on the hospital bed.

When her eyes fluttered open, her brows furrowed until she focused on him. The intensity of her green gaze hit him like a sucker punch to the jaw. Unable to look away, he was entranced by flecks of gold, like bits of glitter, swirling in her irises.

She gasped, trying to sit up. "Oh my God, what did I just see?"

When he pressed her back onto the bed, another protective urge swamped him. Unfortunately, a competing desire to touch her skin again so she'd lift away his darkness nearly won out. He crouched over her, muscles clenching as he fought to keep his hands off of her. He'd never been so close to losing control.

Peter wanted to smooth the worry lines from her forehead. The thought rattled him.

Terror etched upon her fine features as she pressed her soft lips together. "What are you?"

He rubbed his jaw, focusing on her. "What are *you*?"

"I'm an ER doctor."

She eased into a sitting position and brushed away tears. When he stepped away from her, she swayed on the bed, and he caught himself reaching for her again. He dropped his useless, cursed hand.

She pinned him with a heart-stopping stare. "I saw horrible things. What are *you*?"

Blind to everything around him except the woman sitting on the bed, his desperate anger radiated outward in waves.

He gripped her upper arms covered by her lab coat. "Tell me what you saw. Please."

She winced when he didn't let go.

"What. Did. You. See?" He shook her slightly. "What?"

Her lip trembled as tears pooled in her green and gold eyes. Peter froze. Frustration threatened to overpower him as he stood a hair's breadth away from her. He was close enough that a delicate floral scent filled his nostrils, almost enough to distract him.

"I … " She licked her soft lips, commanding his attention. "I saw death."

Chapter 3

Peter shoved her away as though she'd burst into flames. Not possible. All these years, all the hiding. Did she know who he was? *What* he was?

Her lower lip quivered. He stared at her mouth, wanting the touch, wanting her. He leaned forward, pulled as if by an invisible thread. Where did that desire come from?

I have no feelings.

He had to get out of here. His presence meant this woman and the people of this town were in grave danger. Usually he didn't care, but something had changed. He needed to figure out this mess and fast.

"Ahem, excuse me."

He whirled toward the voice behind him.

An older woman stood at the door, eyebrows raised.

He pointed to the bed. "She fainted."

The woman rushed over, putting her hands on the doctor's shoulders. "Dr. Al, are you all right?"

She touched her own cheek with a shaking hand. "Of course. I got a little lightheaded. All fine now, Marcie."

Al. That's an odd name. Allie suits her better, has a bright ring to it. A name full of life, just like Allie.

"And you?" Marcie pinned him with a narrowed glare.

He turned his rarely used charm on the woman. "I feel great."

Smoothing her hair into place, Marcie batted her eyes. "Ahem. Well, there's someone here to see you."

Peter broadened his smile, working hard to distract her from a too-pale Allie, who swayed while sitting on the bed. "Who?" He didn't know anyone in La Grande. *Oh no, not—*

"Your brother, Dante. He's given me all the information for insurance purposes, too. Very helpful, your brother."

Peter groaned. What bogus information had his friend fed the receptionist?

Marcie blinked and then focused on Allie. "Doctor Al, can I bring him in?"

Allie nodded, getting off the bed, but she kept her palm on the edge of the mattress. The pallor of her face nearly matched her white lab coat. What exactly had she seen?

With a doe-eyed expression, Marcie ushered in Dante and exited the room, letting the door swing shut behind her.

His friend pounded Peter on the back. "Peter! You're okay." Dante still spoke with a trace of his Swedish accent, even after all the centuries.

The doctor's eyes widened.

Peter's heart felt like it had dropped to his feet.

Dante could have passed for a blond god straight out of the Scandinavian pantheon. Put a hammer in his hand and he was Thor reincarnated. And, in Peter's opinion, he was also a colossal, swaggering mess of a Don Juan.

Beneath the tailored silk dress shirts and slacks he favored, Dante was a predator, and beautiful women were his preferred prey. Not to kill but to seduce. One of his favorite pastimes was racking up conquests. Peter had to keep Allie away from him.

Too late.

Dante's eerie blue eyes locked onto her. Peter stepped in front of her, but Dante easily shouldered him aside.

"Well, hello, madam." He produced a thousand-kilowatt smile that any Hollywood actor would be proud to own. "Dante Blackstone. You must be the beautiful doctor who saved my brother's life." He offered his massive hand.

Allie stepped back and thrust her hands into her coat pockets. One light brown eyebrow raised, she studied Dante. No two men appeared more *unlike* than the Blackstone "brothers." Was she immune to Dante's charms? Peter had never seen the big man fail. Ever.

The bonehead was probably imagining her body beneath the white coat and scrubs. Peter stepped in front of Allie again, clenching his jaw as he shielded her from Dante's roving eye.

"Are you going to get me out of here, Dante?" Peter slapped him on the arm, hard, refocusing his friend's attention.

"Sure, bro. But I think you need different clothes." Dante flipped up the hem of the pastel green hospital gown before Peter snatched the fabric away. "What've you got under there, my man?" Dante waggled his brows in Allie's direction and grinned at Peter.

Peter's hand curled into a fist. No one would win if he and Dante got into an epic fight, but Peter would do it to get the idiot away from her.

Allison crossed her arms, jaw set, standing toe to toe with both men as they towered over her. Her voice could have cut ice. "Excuse me, this patient should not leave tonight. After that bad of a car wreck, he needs to stay for further observation."

One part of him appreciated her determination. The other part cringed at such foolishness. Allie had no idea who—or rather, what—she was dealing with. If she'd known, she wouldn't have been giving orders. Dante's glacier-blue eyes darkened to black in quick, lethal anger. No one said no to Dante, and he was definitely not someone to cross. Peter had to remove him, and fast.

"Hey, why don't you get me some clothes, *my brother?*" he ground out.

Undistracted, Dante narrowed his eyes as he loomed over Allie. "He's leaving." He leaned closer and flexed his pecs beneath the fine, tailored silk, his usual routine to intimidate humans.

She stood her ground but planted her hands in the coat pockets once again. Peter's primal urge to shield her flared again. He couldn't think straight.

Protect.

He hovered next to the doctor's shoulder, ready to interfere if Dante did something stupid.

Allie took a deep breath. "Here's the deal. Our policy is to observe anyone who has had a severe head injury." At Dante's scowl, her voice rose a notch, her back ramrod straight. "We need to make sure there are no changes in the brain, like swelling."

Dante oozed fury, an emotion totally inappropriate for the situation, but the doctor wouldn't understand that fact. How was she standing there absorbing that much anger? Most humans crumpled beneath the force of his friend's inhumanly augmented charisma and rage.

"If the patient is deemed able to make his own decisions"— Allie turned to Peter—"and, in my opinion, is able to think clearly"—she glared at Dante—"then the patient can sign out of the hospital AMA, or against medical advice."

Dante backed off a step as his expression shifted from irritation to boyish charm. The air in the room cooled several degrees. Peter didn't buy the sweet-as-pie act for a second.

"Well, then, I'll get some clothes and you can sign papers. We're outta here." Air whooshed as Dante exited the room.

Allie's fair skin was much too pale against the dark circles beneath her eyes. Peter would bet she'd held that stiff stance by sheer will. A few pieces of wavy, brown hair curled near her cheeks, begging him to brush back those tendrils. Silence stretched between them.

"Well." He cleared his throat. "Is there some paperwork for me to fill out?"

"Sure is, but first I'd like to know what the hell happened in here earlier."

"In terms of … ?"

"All of it. You recovered way too fast." She tucked a lock of hair behind her ear.

Peter followed the movement. He couldn't stop staring. How sweet would that delicate skin taste?

Damn it all. He dragged his gaze to meet hers.

"And what *was* that when I touched your arm?" Allie pressed her fingertips to her forehead. That gold-flecked, emerald stare rocked him to his core. "Who were all those people? All the deaths? They were horrible."

Her words, like a bucket of cold water, brought him back to reality. Had she seen his actual kills? What *was* she? This could be disastrous.

"Please." He reached out but checked himself as she flinched. He clenched his hand in midair. "You have to tell me what you saw. But not here." He stepped closer until his breath fanned her light brown bangs. "I'll find you, and you will tell me."

It wasn't a question. Fear, narrow suspicion, and then wide-eyed hope flickered across her face.

Dante burst into the room with a bundle of clothes in his arms. "Here you go, Peter. Change and we're good to go."

Allie stepped around the men and exited the room.

Dante followed her movements with a wicked glint in his eyes.

Peter yanked on his clothes. "Come on, man, focus on getting us out of here without more questions being asked."

Dante rubbed his lantern jaw. "There's something about that cute doctor. I'd like to do a physical on *her* one day."

"Shut up," Peter growled as he belted his jeans.

"What? You want her first?"

"Dammit. Just … let's get out of here." They had to leave before the god of thunder did any real damage.

A whiff of sunshine and flowers tormented Peter when she returned.

Dante watched her like a lion stalking a baby impala. Peter's jaw was going to snap, he was grinding his teeth together so hard.

She held out the clipboard. "Here's your AMA form, Mr. Blackstone; if you would sign here. And here." She pointed to Xs on the page. "By signing this form, you are saying that you acknowledge your personal choices are not what your physician recommends for best medical care. As a result, you could come to harm or even die."

Dante, that moron, snorted. Peter glared him into silence.

Clearing her throat, she continued. "Of course, if you have any other problems—worsening headaches, abdominal pain, neck or back pain—please return here at any time."

He signed the form with long, angled slashes that hadn't changed since the 1930s.

Dante raised his eyebrows and grinned behind the doctor's back.

"Thank you for the excellent care," Peter said. He handed the clipboard back by way of a dismissal, and then he and Dante hurried for the exit. He stumbled as the urge to turn around teased him. Temptation won out, and he glanced over his shoulder.

As they were about to exit the emergency department, Marcie flagged them down. "Mr. Dante. You haven't signed the insurance form stating that you will be responsible for any fees beyond what your brother's insurance covers."

Dante closed one eye as he dug in his designer pants pocket and threw a wad of large bills onto the desk. "This should cover his expenses. You have a lovely day, my dear."

Marcie's jaw dropped as Dante winked.

The ER doors whooshed closed behind them.

Peter climbed into the passenger seat of Dante's black Hummer. The mountains above Grande Ronde Hospital blocked the setting sun, casting most of the town in early shadow. Dante's expression might have been difficult to read in the fading light, but Peter didn't mistake the waves of fury rocketing off him.

"*Vad i helvete*, Petey? What the hell? I gotta babysit you on every assignment?"

"Oh, like I planned the wreck? Seriously?" His bones ached, even despite being healed. Each throb along the staple line reminded him of the ER. Of Allie. Her calm, green eyes and her touch like cool water on his long-irritated nerves.

"Hello? Your head injury is worse than I thought." Dante waved his hand in front of Peter's face. "You daydreaming about that doctor? Because I gave her your real cell phone number."

Excitement warred with the practical reality that no human should ever know anything about his kind. That was a stupid move on Dante's part, no matter how much Peter wanted to see her again. After hundreds of years on this Earth, his unhuman friend knew better than to give away any information to an innocent. Dante was living proof that wisdom didn't always come with age.

"You're always supposed to give out fake numbers." Peter rubbed his jaw. "Hell. Doesn't matter. If the hospital calls too much, I'll get a new number. And no, I was not daydreaming. Don't go bringing her into our mess. She's an innocent. The sooner I get out of this town and on to the Boise assignment, the better."

"Job's changed. You're staying here." Dante's hard face revealed no emotion.

"What?" A muscle tightened in Peter's chest. "I can't kill anyone in this town."

"Doesn't matter what you want. Big Boss Jerahmeel must be getting hungry again. Anyway, the person isn't from this town." Dante shot him a tight smirk. "You're to stay here and find the next assignment. They're giving you a hide-and-seek challenge. Unusual. Jerahmeel's got way too much time on his hands. Maybe he's getting tired of the rules he has to follow, tired of killing only criminals to feed his hunger. Who knows? Maybe the lady doctor is your next target," he egged Peter on. "I'm only the messenger on this one."

Dante reached into the back seat and pulled out Peter's duffel bag, wallet, and all identifying information that had been left behind in the totaled SUV. Dante might be dense, but at least his 300-year-old friend knew how to cover tracks.

"I assumed the police kept all of the stuff after an accident," Peter said.

"That's what the police thought. There are advantages to our super speed, you know. Poor local constables never knew I took all their evidence." He tapped Peter's wallet. "I also put enough in there for another vehicle, and there are nice hotels in town. Maybe you should take a bubble bath and relax. Go get a massage. You've had a long day."

"Uh, you find anything else in the car?"

"Like this?" He dug under the front seat and handed over the knife. It was still flecked with dried blood from the accident. "Disgusting, bro. And you know you're not supposed to be able to take this off."

Peter fished out a shirt from his duffel bag and cleaned off the knife. Relief spread like melting butter through his torso, and his muscles relaxed. "It was hard to remove, but I had to hide it from the innocents. I'm just glad that no one got hurt. Hell, it feels good to have it back. How sick is that?"

"Our weapons are a part of us, bro."

"I know. Disgusting what it makes us do. What being Indebted mandates we do."

"Tasty treats for Jerahmeel." Dante flashed a grin that didn't reach his ice-blue eyes.

Jerahmeel, their boss. Satan in human form, who thrived off of the criminal blood when Peter and Dante or any others like them plunged their knives into the bodies of their kills. The twelve-inch, unnaturally sharp blades channeled criminals' insanity, wickedness, and cruelty—the highest form of evil power—directly into their overlord. Peter's entire, disgusting existence boiled down to the knife, a constant reminder of the sacrifice he'd made so many years ago, the last time he was truly human. The knife glowed green in his hands.

His big Swedish friend ran a meaty hand through rumpled blond hair. "The knife *wants* you. How'd you get it away?"

"Wasn't easy, but I needed to hide it more than I wanted it attached to me. For a while."

"For a while? Who are you kidding? Our damned weapons complete us."

Peter slid the knife into a new holster he pulled from the duffel bag. "For a guy in the same predicament as me, you're a real prick."

"Bet you wish you could figure out how to keep it off forever."

"You have no idea."

He strapped the holster back onto his lower leg. Relief and completeness flowed over him. He both loved and hated how the knife felt back in its place. How screwed up could one man be?

A few students were walking home in the cool evening air as the Hummer's route took them by Eastern Oregon University. Peter studied each person on the street. Which one would be his next quarry? Would it be the tall guy with combat boots and a bold sneer? Or how about the young lady who darted glances in every direction as she hurried down the sidewalk? Thanks to his knife-guided radar for criminals, everyone was a suspect.

"When's all this going to stop?" Peter ran his hands over his head, wincing as he grazed the staples. That gash in his scalp was a doozy, even for him. It would take a day or so to completely heal. Maybe that was why he still had a sense of Allie. He detected her presence, as though she sat silently a few feet away. *Strange.* "You've done this longer than me, Dante. When's our last assignment going to be?"

"Dude, you know the rule. When you're an Indebted, you have to perform the Meaningful Kill to get out of the contract. Obviously neither of us has gotten it done yet."

One of their contract stipulations restricted them to killing criminals, humans whose deeds were so despicable, they had amassed a tremendous amount of negative energy. That's what

Jerahmeel wanted. Oh, he could consume the energy of innocent souls, of course, but that meal didn't satisfy him, didn't give the power he craved. Thus the rule.

Peter fingered the knife handle, reassuring himself that the blade rested securely in the sheath. "Why haven't we gotten the Meaningful Kill? What about the wars? Prowling the streets, tracking murderers? How are those not meaningful?"

"Yeah, doesn't make sense. I guess there's one out there that counts more. I guess the number's different for each of us, or maybe it's a sick game the big boss plays. But what're you in a hurry for? You've got the whole world at your feet, bro. Only the world doesn't know."

Peter stared out the window. "You know why I want to be done. Same as you. What'd you leave behind for this job?"

Silence.

"Exactly."

Dante pulled up to a hotel near the interstate. "Well, we're stuck in this life, such as it is. Might as well make the most of it." He grinned. "I might stop off at one of those gentlemen's clubs on the way to Boise and make the most of my life tonight … and maybe someone else's. Why be here forever if you can't have some fun?"

Peter stepped out, shut the Hummer door, and watched Dante speed off into the night. He got along well enough with his friend, but Peter needed to get to work. Alone. First item on the agenda was to flush out his assignment. Second, sink the hungry knife blade into the next assignment and hold out hope it was his Meaningful Kill. Last but not least, avoid thinking about a certain lovely doctor. Easy enough.

Groaning as he hefted the duffel bag, he was reminded that, despite being not completely human, he still felt aches and pains like any old man. After nearly a hundred years, even someone with Peter's strength needed time and rest to recover.

Chapter 4

Allison grimaced against the cold wind biting through her thin scrub pants and pulled her jacket tight. She hurried into Wally's Diner in downtown La Grande. A renovated train depot, Wally's had the best breakfast in town. She and her sister met for breakfast one Saturday every month. No matter how tired she felt, she never missed this time. After their father's death years ago, Sarah had been her only support, and Allison had never forgotten that.

"Hi, Al." Her older sister's head bobbed from a booth next to the windows, her light brown hair brushing her shoulders.

"Hey, Sarah. Been waiting long?"

"No, just got here. Spring break's this week and Quincy's already stir crazy. Her father gets to entertain her until a play date at noon. He's helping her pick an outfit." Sarah raised her eyebrows. "It's good for him to stay up on the latest fashions for six-year-old girls."

"I can imagine. By the time they're finished, everything will be out of the closet."

"And not a thing to wear."

Ah, her brother-in-law officiating her niece's impromptu fashion show. Allison smiled. Quincy turned her tough, cop father into a pile of mush every time.

Chuckling, they gave their breakfast orders to the waitress. Allison eased back into the vinyl booth as her neck and shoulder muscles relaxed.

"Bad night in the ER?"

Allison took her hair out of its clip and then pulled the hair off of her shoulders. "Yeah, not great, that's for sure."

"Another vision?"

"Worst one yet." She rubbed her hand on her pant leg.

"It wasn't but a month ago you had your last one. They're coming closer together. And they're worse? What happened?"

"EMS brought this man into the ER, bad wreck off the interstate. The guy's totally unconscious, on a backboard, seems like maybe he's had internal injuries and possible head trauma. Very bad."

The waitress brought over their drinks.

Sarah wrapped both hands around her steaming coffee cup and leaned forward.

Allison inhaled the aroma from her mug. "I go to examine him and notice a little tingle in my fingertips, weird vibrations coming through the gloves. I try not to think about it and keep working on the guy. After he comes back from the CAT scan, he wakes right up … like goes from a Glasgow Coma Scale of three to perfectly fine in under an hour."

"Is that normal?"

"No. Actually, I've never seen anyone recover that fast." She rubbed the goose bumps on her arms. "So he jumps up, I grab him, and, *boom*, a vision."

"What'd you see?" Sarah sipped her coffee. "Besides the usual."

Her sister didn't meet her eyes.

Allison stared at the steam coming from her drink. "This one was different. It was all death, but not the guy's death, or at least I don't think so. This vision was like a bizarre horror flick with dead people everywhere. I was *inside* the vision this time. Shaking hands with a scary man surrounded by smoke. Then I killed people with a knife, or the patient did. Every time I close my eyes, the horrible images are right there. If I can't figure out how to forget what I saw, I think I'll lose my mind."

Sarah placed a hand on Allison's arm. At first Allison tensed, then finally relaxed with a deep sigh when she did not receive a vision of her sister's death. Maybe one day Allison wouldn't live in fear. One day.

The waitress set steaming breakfast plates in front of them. The crispy bacon and cheese omelet served as a sad reminder of weekend family breakfasts twenty years ago.

"What do you think it all means?" her sister asked.

Allison cut off a corner of toast with her fork. "I wish I knew. I guess he's a dead man. They all die, everyone whose vision I see. But I witnessed all these other deaths, too. Maybe the patient killed all those people. Maybe I tapped into his subconscious because of the head injury. I don't know. All I know is that I won't be able to sleep. The visions were worse than any nightmare I could imagine."

"Did the guy know what you saw?"

"Oddly, yes, I think so. I hit the floor because the vision was so intense. When he helped me up, he asked *what* I was." And his eyes had bored right into her soul. "Then he wanted to know what I'd seen. Spooky. In the past, the other person has always been oblivious to the fact that I'm getting a vision. They sense nothing."

"That's strange. Think you'll see him again?" Sarah tapped her chin.

"I don't think he's from around here." Allison chewed a bite of the buttery toast. "So, no, I expect he's long gone, especially given how much he wanted to get out of the ER. You know what's kind of strange? There's a faint echo of something different in my mind. Like someone whispering across the room. I can barely hear the words."

"You ever had that before?"

"Not that I recall, no." She sighed.

"Well, do you think you should've told him what you saw?"

A lump formed in her throat. "No, I never want to tell anyone what I see." Allison nibbled on her bacon. "I told Dad and it ruined our entire lives."

"That wasn't your fault, Al." The topic was familiar yet they trod lightly.

"It's my fault he died." Out the window, the pale blue sky peeked from between the early spring clouds. Allison couldn't enjoy the view. "That's what Mom kept telling me, especially when she got into the pills."

Her mother had said that and much more. Not only did her mother blame Allison for her father's death, she reinforced what a defective human being Allison had become. Despite Allison's efforts to help her mother, the woman who had given birth and raised her had then demoralized her. Ripped away Allison's hope in her own humanity. For a short while, she thought her name was "freak" because her mother had used the term so often. The damage was precise, cruel, and long-lasting. So far, her mother's predictions that Allison would never have a loving family of her own had come true.

Sarah cleared her throat. "Take it from your family member who didn't have a nervous breakdown. You didn't cause Dad's death. Not even close. You reported what you saw." She sipped her coffee. "Anyway, it doesn't sound like you'll be seeing this guy again. I'd try and let this one go."

Around the painful lump in her throat, Allison managed to choke down a breakfast that had lost all flavor. All she wanted in this world was to be rid of her useless, sick power. She wanted a normal life, to love a normal man, and maybe have a family. But that wasn't going to happen as long as she continued in her role as the angel of death.

After leaving Wally's, she drove north out of town to the base of a low mountain and pulled into the garage of her one-story craftsman home. Even home didn't produce the usual peaceful feeling.

When she entered the house, Ivy, her massive, fawn-colored dog, came careening around the kitchen, knocking one barstool over in her haste to reach Allison. Hugging the enormous dog's head to her hip, she petted her behind the ears and avoided getting thwacked by her whip-like tail, which oscillated at a ridiculously high rate. A mix between Great Dane and Golden Retriever, Ivy had no clue what destructive power she wielded. Although Ivy was friendly, she also scared away bears outside the house and made for an intimidating running partner.

An unexpected chill ran down Allison's back as she considered who or what could hide in the forest without her knowledge. Unbidden, the image of Peter Blackstone's intense face loomed in her mind, followed by that faint sense of him. Rubbing her chilled arms, she recalled his promise to see her again and her stomach flopped. Once the prickly sensation abated, she righted the kitchen stool. She wanted nothing more than to go to sleep, but Ivy picked up her leash in her mouth and, with a pitiful expression worthy of an Oscar, dropped it at Allison's feet. Ivy knew how to work her over hard.

"All right, Ivy. I can go a few miles today." She clipped on Ivy's leash and headed into the late March morning, led by her happy, giant dog. Even a pleasant stroll in the crisp air didn't distract her from dwelling on a certain patient's dark eyes.

· · ·

After walking to the car dealership Saturday morning, Peter purchased a used pickup truck. His mood had gone from foul to downright nasty. He'd been up all night, wanting to go back to the ER and see Allie. That weird, whispering sense of her continued as well, just beyond his range of hearing.

All of his injuries had healed overnight, as expected. Only residual fatigue remained, and that symptom should be gone by evening.

He wanted to leave town. He wanted to be anything but the killer he was. Who cared what Dante said? This … existence … was no life.

Driving around town, Peter scanned the area halfheartedly. He saw no one suspicious, only pleasant folks running errands, going to work, performing mundane activities. It was entirely possible that Dante left him here to cool his heels so he could take all the credit for the Boise assignment. Then again, the instructions seemed to come from the big boss, and Peter couldn't argue with that kind of mandate.

In another life, Peter might have lived in a place like La Grande. According to the information at the hotel, the small college town had started as an agricultural hub; gold and silver mines in the late 1800s caused a boom. Above the hospital to the west were ridges of low mountains that gave way to central Oregon's high desert, and across a valley to the east rose the higher Wallowa Mountains. He'd love to hide forever in a place like that.

Who was he fooling? He could never hide. Not for long.

He breathed in the clean, crisp air as he wound through a residential area. Inviting porches and backyard jungle gyms conjured images of family. He'd come close to having a family years ago. So close.

And what about Allie? He'd tortured himself last night, thinking of her in his arms, protecting her. From what?

People like me.

The horror and disgust in her eyes when she'd touched him pretty much summed up his entire existence. But shame … now that was a new emotion. He hadn't experienced anything other than anger for more years than he could count.

Whatever she had done, Allie had woken something inside of him with her touch. And what about their connection? He had a weird echo in his mind, like a weak radio signal bleeding through a stronger one. He couldn't make out details, but the tingly sensation felt like … her. He wanted more of that connection. More of her.

Since Claire, he hadn't been with another woman. Guilt stopped him every time. Only when he'd connected with Allie had he experienced attraction once more.

He braked at an intersection. As he glanced up the cross street, a movement caught his eye.

A stocky man with a crew cut and wearing a leather jacket glared at Peter. The man picked at his head with a finger and glanced around, as if on alert. He pulled the jacket collar up, hunched his shoulders, and stared at Peter with narrowed eyes. Then the man jumped in a car and sped away. With his stalker's sense on high alert, Peter turned down the street and focused on the man. The car disappeared in the dense residential area, but Peter kept searching. Something wasn't right. Was this man the next kill? The Meaningful Kill?

He fought the impulse to run after the target. Although being an Indebted meant that Peter could move almost faster than a human eye could follow, that speed—and his strength—had finite limits. Best to complete his recovery from the accident and avoid drawing any attention by staying in the truck.

Over the next several hours, he scoured neighborhoods, determined to find the man. He kept driving well into the night, dark thoughts his only companions.

By the time he pulled into the hotel parking lot after a long day of finding nothing, his frustration level had risen to a new high. He couldn't keep doing this … job. He had always hated what he had to do, but after seeing the horror in Allie's eyes, he despised how his life had spiraled into this ugliness.

She represented possibilities and hope—two things he neither deserved nor wanted to consider.

Peter's current grim existence baffled him. Wasn't it only yesterday that he'd become this unhuman contract killer and mere hours ago that he made the ultimate sacrifice? In reality, it had been more than seventy years. All for what purpose? Nothing.

There was one person who could help him, one person who'd ever completed his contract for the boss man. One tale of success in anyone's memory.

Barnaby.

Peter shoved the plastic card into the hotel room's door lock and walked straight to his computer. He pulled up an encrypted file. If Jerahmeel knew he had this number, Peter would be worse than dead. Thumbing on his cell phone, he dialed.

"Barnaby? It's Peter."

A male answered, his cracked voice quavering. "Well, hello, my boy! Please speak up. My hearing isn't overly good."

Peter dropped onto the stiff sofa bed. "I need some advice."

"Oh, ho, I have plenty of opinions. Mayhap not informed ones, but I have them."

Peter smiled as Barnaby's accent slid back and forth between contemporary English and the English of his Elizabethan youth. "I met a human who has some … interesting abilities."

"Like of the flesh?" Barnaby chortled.

"Do you think I'd call you for *that*?"

"Okay, my boy, do you require counsel regarding an assignment?"

Peter propped his feet on the coffee table. "No. I'm calling about someone I came into contact with here. I think she knows what I am."

Dead silence.

"What do you mean?"

"I think she saw the wars, the assignments, the kills … everything."

"And what did you see?"

Besides Allie crumpled on the hospital floor, horror in her eyes? "I watched her suffer, and for a second, I felt human again, like all the pain had been lifted away. What the hell was that?"

"Oh my, I believe you've found yourself a Ward."

"A what?"

"A Ward. I met one once. Sweet lady."

"What are they?" Peter rubbed his jaw.

"Wards are rare. They are people who can see death in one form or another."

"And that's what we are. Death."

"That's what *you* are, Peter. I'm out of the business, remember?"

"Yeah, lucky you." He grimaced. "Are Wards dangerous?"

"Depends on who you ask. They can be dangerous to themselves, as in the case of your lady friend taking the vapors when she touches you." Barnaby coughed for a minute. "But our kind can be dangerous to the Ward."

Peter gripped the phone harder. "How?"

"They're like radar. If they come into contact with us, they can see what we are. That's unacceptable to some of our ilk, especially Jerahmeel. He would do anything to eliminate the Ward."

"Eliminate?" Peter's blood turned to ice.

"Yes, my boy. If you've found a Ward, not only can you hurt her with the visions, but there are some who will stop at nothing to kill her. Your boss loves control and power, and Wards take that away. Does anyone else know what she is?"

"I don't think she even knows. She should be safe." His heart slowed to a normal pace. "Where do they come from?"

"No one knows, or at least no one I've talked to. But in my travels over the years, I've heard about a Ward popping up every so often. I do wonder if there is some flaw in the blood every century or so that creates a Ward."

The knife blade in his leg sheath clunked against the tabletop when Peter crossed his ankles. "Know how to make the visions stop?"

Barnaby snorted. "Rather inconvenient for the lady to swoon every time you have contact with her, hmm?"

"Something like that. I'm only curious."

"Sure you are. Well, to answer your question, yes, I think these visions verily can be blocked."

"And?" Peter pressed the phone to his ear.

"When I met my Ward, I nearly killed her. It was 1863, and Susan was an old widow living in Virginia. She was a wonderful boon companion for a few years. I afforded her some protection and helped keep her property cleared and fields sown."

"That sounds nice, but what about blocking the visions?"

"Oh yes, blocking. It takes practice, but it can be done." He coughed for a few moments. "You ever have a secret? ... Never mind, your whole life is a secret." His wheezing laughter rattled over the phone. "Well, you have to learn to hold in your thoughts and emotions when you come into contact with the other person. Much like holding in a sneeze, but it gets easier with practice. And the Ward has to be prepared to block any visions you can't hold back."

"How does a Ward block the visions?"

"First of all, if you're going to go down this path, you'll need to tell the Ward who you are and what the visions represent."

"I can't do that. Besides, I don't know if I'll even see her again."

"Keep telling yourself that. If you don't explain what she is experiencing, then you can make the Ward overwrought, and the visions might kill her if she's unprepared." He honked his nose and sniffed. "Pardon me. Allergies. Once a Ward knows what she's seeing, it's easier to hold the visions back. Susan and I managed. She blocked her visions of me by being overly polite."

"Excuse me? I don't understand. Polite?"

"Yes, she said it was like going to a social event such as a wedding where she had to talk with people she didn't like. She would have to be polite and put up a mental barrier to keep her feelings hidden."

"And that worked?" Maybe there was a chance he could touch Allie without killing her.

"In a manner of speaking. When Susan sensed the visions coming, she would think about a stiff social event. She managed to get the barrier up to heavily filter the images. At least she understood what the images were and wasn't overwhelmed by them."

"Interesting."

Barnaby wheezed for a moment. "Hope that works for you, my boy."

"Thanks, me too." Peter paused. "Can I ask you one more question?"

"Surely," came Barnaby's voice, gravelly with age.

Peter planted his feet on the floor and leaned forward. "How'd you do it? Get out of your contract?"

"I can't tell. Trade secret, very unpopular with our lord Jerahmeel. The fewer Indebted, the hungrier and more desperate he gets for souls. But despite his twisted ways, he is bound by at least a few rules."

"What are they?"

"No one knows exactly, but I have made a few accurate guesses over the centuries. The rules were set so many years ago."

"Before you?"

"Oh yes, well before me." He blew his nose again. "Let's see, if I remember correctly, Jerahmeel became what he is today sometime in the thirteenth century."

"I've never heard this. Why? How?"

"Some kind of religious holocaust back then. Wiped out his family, made him what he is today. Details are scarce, but I do know part of the deal was that if he wanted to stay strong and immortal, he had a few rules to follow. He can only come so close to crossing that line. That's how I got out."

"How?"

"I'm sorry, my boy. My final oath was to never share those details. Let me just say that my lovely wife, Jane, God rest her beautiful soul, was my inspiration. Now I've said too much already, my boy."

Barnaby's deceased wife had been the love of the recent, natural portion of his life.

"But what about now?" Peter continued. "How do you feel now that you've reached the end of your own life?"

"Breaking the contract and becoming mortal was completely worth the risk and the pain and the loss of immortality. Don't get me wrong. My joints ache, the pate is bald, and I can't remember my last decent erection. I'm a defective mess. But I get to live a *life* to its natural conclusion. There's a satisfaction in finally moving on."

Peter shoved his hand through his hair, cursing when he hit the line of staples. "Yeah, I see what you mean."

"You'll get there, my boy."

"Thanks, old man. I appreciate it."

"I'd say any time, but at some point in the future, that won't be the case." Barnaby coughed again. "But as long as I'm here, I'm always happy to help."

Chapter 5

At noon on Monday during her next twenty-four-hour shift, Allison picked up the doctor's workstation phone and dialed Peter Blackstone's contact number. Her heart thudded, and she had to take a deep breath. On the second ring, he picked up.

"Hello?" His low voice sent chills up her arms. She relaxed her death grip on the phone.

"Mr. Blackstone, this is Dr. La Croix from the Grande Ronde ER. I was calling to check on you after your accident."

"Do you call all of your patients?"

She rocked back on her heels at the gruff reply. "Uh no, but if they're seriously ill or injured or they leave AMA, then we try make sure they're doing okay. My personal policy is to call all AMA patients myself on my next shift."

"Oh. Yes, then I'm fine."

Stammering a reply, she struggled to salvage the conversation and maintain her professionalism. "Um, all right. If you have any other problems or notice new symptoms, please feel free to return to the ER. You can always be re-evaluated."

The silence stretched out.

Is he still on the phone?

"There's this one problem you might be able to help with," he finally said.

"Sure." She gulped. "What's the problem?"

"These staples are driving me crazy. Can you take them out?"

"Possibly. It's a little early to remove them, but if you want to stop in today, I'll see what I can do."

"Until then."

The line went dead. Allison's hands shook. She was going to see him again. She shivered, anticipating his dark eyes, his touch.

Almost craved it, almost felt it, which was bizarre, not to mention unprofessional.

Another horrible thought occurred to her. What if he truly knew about her visions? Would he reveal the secret? She pressed her fingers to the bridge of her nose and tried to concentrate on the chart in front of her.

That afternoon, Allison put the finishing touches on a bright red forearm cast for an unlucky, eleven-year-old trampoline victim. He preened beneath the attention of the nurses, who signed his cast with lots of XOXOs. Allison smiled at his mother, who, with two other young boys in tow, returned a weary grin. She bet it wouldn't be the last trip this mother made to the ER with an adventurous kid.

And throughout the encounter, Allison managed to keep one eye on the security monitor for the reception area.

The family had just signed off on the paperwork when the ER doors whooshed open on the monitor.

Allison's heart jumped. She peeked down the hall.

Her niece dodged past Sarah into the reception area, stopped abruptly, and planted her toes on the line painted perpendicular to the reception desk.

"Hi, Marcie!" Pigtails askew, the girl waved at the ER receptionist.

The older woman smiled. "Quincy! How's my favorite princess?"

Quincy unselfconsciously fluffed her satin and lace dress and dropped into a curtsey. "Sierra had a birthday party today. I won a prize." She pointed to her sparkly wand. "Um, is Auntie Al busy?" Her toes stayed glued to the line.

Marcie called out, "Doctor Al? Princess here to see you."

Straightening her white coat as she rounded the corner, Allison opened her arms for Quincy to run to her. Careful not to touch Quincy's skin, Allison patted the back of her niece's poufy outfit.

"Let's see the dress. Now, what kind of princess are you?" Allison played along to the delight of the twirling, preening six-year-old.

"Fairy princess!"

"Yes, but where are your wings?"

Momentarily stymied, Quincy recovered and motioned for Allison to lean down. She whispered, "They're invisible wings. Only true princesses can see them."

"Oh, then I must not be a true princess." Allison pulled a sad face.

Sarah hid her laugh behind a cough.

Quincy straightened. "Hmm. Then I will make you a princess for today." She tapped Allison on the arm with her wand.

Allison oozed gracious surprise. "Hey, now I can see your wings! They're so very beautiful. Thank you, fairy princess."

Quincy twirled on her toes, giggling, as satin and crinoline swished out around her.

"Okay, Miss Fairy Princess, you got your wish to say hi to Auntie Al. Now it's time to get home for dinner," Sarah said.

"You heard your mother." At Quincy's moue of unhappiness, Allison announced in a passably dramatic voice, "Let us part ways with princess kisses." She placed air kisses on either side of Quincy's head, much to the young girl's ecstasy.

Quincy hugged Allison again. "Bye, Auntie Al!"

Senses on sudden alert, Allison's heart skipped a beat, and her breath caught when she saw the figure standing in the open doorway. Peter had slipped into the ER reception area and was taking in Quincy's antics with a crooked smile softening his dark gaze. She hadn't seen him truly smile before. His face was transformed into something even more handsome.

Sarah raised her eyebrow with an impish smirk. Her older sister's eyes narrowed on Peter until Quincy tugged her out the doors.

He motioned toward the ER doors. "Busy day?"

Breathe, Allison. Ignoring Marcie's slack-jawed expression at the jeans-clad man, she laughed. "Busy if you're a fairy princess, I suppose."

Peter gestured to his head. All she saw was his short, black hair, neatly brushed to the side. "Can you work on a non-princess for a staple removal?"

"It just so happens I don't have any patients here right now."

"You mean it's quiet?" He frowned at Marcie and Allison's twin gasps of horror. "What?"

"You're not supposed to say that word in here." Allison crossed her arms. "If you say it, bad things will happen."

Marcie crossed her arms in mirror image and nodded.

Peter raised his arms. "Sorry, I don't know the rules. Will you still take out my staples? I promise not to bleed out or have a sudden emergency."

With a grin, Allison waved him into an exam room and pulled out a vinyl chair, motioning for him to sit. She opened a cabinet to retrieve gauze and a staple removal kit. The low-level vibration of his mind echoed more persistently in her head.

When she turned around, she ran into Peter's chest and jumped back. No visions. His flannel shirt prevented skin-to-skin contact, thank goodness. He remained close, staring down at her in the awkward silence. The room was much too small and too warm.

Seriously, what was she doing? She had no business, personally or professionally, thinking of him as anything but a patient. Besides, if he knew what a freak of humanity she truly was, he'd run far away and stay gone.

"Uh, if you can sit, I can get to your staples more easily that way."

He settled onto the chair, his eyes never leaving her face.

His thigh muscles bunched under the denim as he sat, the sight making her mouth go dry. A spicy, masculine scent mixed with his still-damp hair. She wanted to bury her nose at the nape of his neck and inhale.

Damn it, keep it professional.

With a deep sigh, she pulled on gloves and refused to think of anything besides removing the staples. She couldn't even come up with small talk, so the staples clinked too loudly as they dropped into the metal basin.

"Interesting," she murmured.

Peter turned his head and glanced up at her.

"You've healed extremely fast. You can barely tell there was ever a laceration."

Clink, clink.

When she finished, she circled around and peered at his face. "And your bruises are gone, too. I don't understand; that's too quick to heal." Allison frowned as she brushed his cheekbone with her gloved hand.

Seizing her hand with a deep growl, he lurched to his feet, knocking over the metal tray in the process. He held her with a firm grip, but he didn't hurt her.

She struggled for air, her fingertips tingling, even through the gloves. Eyes level with his collarbone, she leaned back, desperate for personal space.

Damn it. Not another vision. It's too soon.

She tugged at her hand, but he held fast, dragging her to within mere inches of his chest. Waves of heat washed over her until sweat prickled between her breasts.

A muscle in his jaw jumped. "What did you see the other day when I was here?" The tense, desperate tone of his voice caught her off-guard.

She studied his broad chest where the buttons on his shirt strained against his rapid breaths. Gulping, she glanced up at him. "I saw a man who should've been dead, or at least critically injured, in a car accident wake up and walk out of here like nothing had happened."

"That's not what I meant," he said, tightening his grip. "When you touched my arm, what did you see?"

She licked her lips and froze while he stared at her mouth. "I saw death." She met his dark brown gaze. "And it was awful."

Peter dropped her hand as though he'd been scalded.

She staggered back a step.

His mouth compressed into an angry line. "I need to talk with you." He glanced around the room. "Not here."

"I'm not sure that's—"

"Please." The word seemed torn from him.

An ache twisted in her chest as compassion overcame her fear.

His intense, dark gaze bore into her eyes. "I know what you are."

Her heart flopped. "What did you say?" Heck, even she didn't know *what* she was. Or what was wrong with her. She simply saw things. How could he know more about her abilities than she did?

"I think I can help you stop seeing these ... images."

Allison rocked back on her heels. He could stop her visions? How was that even possible? All the heartache she'd endured, predicting people's deaths. That constant, paralyzing terror that she would predict more of her family members' deaths. How could she pass up the chance to be normal?

She considered his strong face, the warmth of his body reaching across the space between them. She didn't know this man. Could she trust him? Her chart told her there was something fundamentally different about him. Her non-clinical instincts insisted that he was a decent guy.

When she boiled it all down, who the hell cared? She was toxic to her fellow human beings the way things stood now. If someone could fix her twisted gift, she couldn't pass up that opportunity.

Bottom line: if he could help her, she had to trust this man.

"All right, I'll talk with you. As long as you can make all of this stop." She gestured toward her head. "I work twenty-four-hour shifts, so I'll be done after eight tomorrow morning."

He watched her for a moment, then cleared his throat. "Until tomorrow. Thank you for taking out the staples." The door swung closed behind him.

As the silence enveloped her, she stood in the exam room, feeling bereft. And fascinated. And horrified.

Peter Blackstone knew her secret.

A strange echo of him pinged in the back of her mind, the sensation reassuring, like someone else was on her side.

With a shake of her head, she washed her hands and headed back out to continue her shift.

Chapter 6

Leaning against the wall outside the ER, Peter turned his head as the doors slid open and Allie emerged. The air caught in his chest. He hadn't realized how much he'd anticipated seeing her again. Excitement percolated. Or was it that whisper of her in his mind? No matter. This wasn't the time to have any personal interest in a woman. Not for something like him.

"Did my 'Q' word cause problems last night?"

He kept pace as she walked slowly across the parking lot. She clutched her jacket closed against the cool morning air.

"Thankfully, for your sake, no problems." She paused at her driver's side door and smiled.

He hadn't seen a smile like that for too many years to count. Something twisted in a bittersweet way in his heart until he had to clear his throat. "I'd like to go somewhere and talk. If that's still okay with you."

She slowly unwrapped her hands from the jacket and took a deep breath.

He held his own breath.

After a minute, she let out a sigh. It sounded like sweet music to his ears.

"Okay."

Trying to strike a balance between friend and stalker, he said, "If we're going to discuss your special powers, we should be somewhere no one can see or hear us."

"Agreed." Her brow furrowed as she peered up at the cool morning sky.

He clenched his jaw, willing patience.

Her small hands clutched a satchel which triggered unbidden images of those hands on him. Primal craving shocked him as it erupted with unexpected force. He wanted Allie in his arms. Badly. The mere thought was completely inappropriate, magical even, given his occupation and his bizarre existence. How could he be with anyone in his current state? With effort, he focused on what she was saying.

"If you want to follow me, we can talk at my place." Her pulse jumped at the base of her throat.

He wanted his lips there.

Not now. Focus. "I'll be right behind you."

Despite his flaming desire, he refused to betray the trust she'd placed in him. He strode back to his truck. Glancing around the parking lot, he spied a man in a sedan near the far entrance. Peter looked down to put the key in the ignition, and when he raised his head, the vehicle was gone.

The beauty of the low mountains that rose parallel to the county road on the way to Allie's soothed his wretched soul. He followed her vehicle onto a dirt lane that ended at a one-story house, surrounded by pine trees and tucked into the base of the mountain. When he got out of his truck, he turned in a circle and breathed in the fresh scent of the evergreens. The view of the valley and snow-capped Wallowa Mountains turned something heavy in his chest. All this—the house, the trees, the view, the woman—he could never have.

Her welcoming front porch, adorned with a swing and bamboo wind chimes, all but folded him in in a warm embrace. He could almost see the white curtains of his first house fluttering in the light summer breeze from the open windows. He could hear echoes of children playing hoops and hopscotch on the sidewalk in the warm evening air. His wife, Claire, waved through the front window as he returned home. When he worked to make out the details of her face, panic flooded him. Damn it, he'd lost the memory of Claire's face.

He slammed the truck door and followed Allie into the garage.

"Coming?" She had her hand on the garage door switch.

Shaking his head to free memories of a life long gone, he trailed after her into the kitchen. When she flipped on the lights and put her bag down on the counter, a barking hulk launched itself at her.

Peter stepped in to intervene, but she put one foot back and braced for impact with perfect timing. Her smile improved even his cynical nature as she pointed to the floor. The dog dropped to Allie's feet, tongue lolling and tail thumping.

The beast focused on him, growled once, and sniffed his shoes and hands. The dog gave a single bark and then licked his hand, satisfied.

"Ivy likes you," Allie said.

"Ivy?"

"Actually, it's I.V. I got her in med school. It was my own inside joke." She shrugged. "Ivy doesn't realize how ginormous she's become. She thinks she's still a puppy."

He didn't have to reach far to pet Ivy behind the ears. The dog rolled her eyes in ecstasy and the thumping on the floor increased in tempo.

"Oh, and be careful, she's got enough Great Dane in her to make her tail a lethal weapon."

Ivy whacked him on the leg with said appendage.

Allie grinned. "Coffee?"

"Sounds great." He petted Ivy while he inhaled the rich aroma of coffee and home, such a wonderful combination of scents.

"Where are you from?" she asked unexpectedly, her calm, green eyes pinning him.

"Ohio. Columbus area."

"Lots of ice and snow there in wintertime."

"Very true." He'd shoveled out the front walkway many times. "Isn't it cold here, though?"

"Sure, but it's drier."

When she handed him the coffee cup, he didn't miss how she pulled her hand back before he could come into contact with her skin.

He enjoyed a few sips and then cleared his throat. "Uh, could we sit down and talk?"

She led him into the living room and sat at the end of the couch. Ivy flopped at her feet. At Allie's gesture, he sank into a wingback chair with a sigh. For a moment, as he ran his hands over the curling armrests, he was transported back to his own living room years ago.

He forced himself back to the present. "These visions. What happens when you get them?"

She wrapped her hands around the steaming mug and took a sip. "It hurts." When she paused, he nodded in encouragement. "I don't really know when they will come, but I apparently now will get a warning tingle in my fingers, like with you the other day." She stared down into the cup. "Sometimes not, and then the vision hits out of the blue."

"What does it feel like?"

"Imagine a million volts of electricity, mainlined."

Allie in pain. Unacceptable. "What do you see?"

"Death. It's always about death."

She reached down and petted Ivy's head. When a sad frown creased her fine features, he gripped the chair arm to keep his hand from smoothing her brow.

He placed his coffee mug on a coaster and leaned forward, resting his forearms on his knees. "When did you start having these visions?"

"I was ten. My dad came home from work. When I went to hug him, it felt like I'd been sucker-punched in the stomach." She stared blankly into space, rubbing her flat abdomen. "I had such an awful vision of him, withered, in pain, and dying. I ran to the bathroom to throw up. When Dad came to check on me, as soon as he touched me, the visions came back, even worse."

Peter fought an overwhelming urge to pull her into his arms. The glistening in her eyes tore right through his chest, but he sat immobile.

Don't feel anything. Not with this woman.

"Of course, I had no idea what happened. When Dad asked, I told him everything. I didn't know back then *not* to tell anyone what I saw. He and Mom were horrified. They probably figured I was bipolar or something." Allie's jaw set and her lips thinned. "Dad was dead of pancreatic cancer three months later."

"That's terrible."

"Yes, it was. But what was worse was having my mother blame me for killing him."

Peter rocked back in the chair. How could her mother say that? "You didn't kill him."

"I didn't make him better, did I? What use are these stupid visions if I can't prevent what's coming?"

He had an idea of the pain her "gift" caused. "What happened after he died?"

"Mom had a nervous breakdown. Sarah, my older sister, and I took care of Mom ourselves." She brushed a stray piece of hair away from her cheek.

"Where is your mom now?"

"She kept spiraling downward and got onto Xanax and Oxycontin for anxiety and pain. Then she started binge drinking. Sarah and I tried to help her, but I don't think Mom wanted to live. Every single day, she told me in no uncertain terms exactly how I had killed the love of her life, and how much she hated me."

"You must have realized how unfair that was." How had Allie kept from breaking down herself under that kind of emotional onslaught?

"Doesn't matter if it's fair. That's how it was." She crossed her arms over her chest. "Sarah went to college, I graduated high school and left home, and Mom killed herself on pills and alcohol."

"Brutal."

She brought her knees to her chest and rested her head on her knees. "Yep, but Sarah and I stuck together. At least she's never accused me of killing anyone. And she always tells me she's not scared that I'll have a vision of her one day."

"But are *you* scared?" He refused to look away, trying to tear down a little of her wall. "Of seeing the death of someone you care for?"

"Wouldn't anyone be scared? How messed up is that?"

At the quiver in her voice, he fought another urge to haul her into his arms.

Tapping a finger on the rim of the coffee cup, she sighed. "You know, I even tried dating in college. Things were great until I got a vision of a boyfriend. I kept telling myself that seeing his death was ridiculous, that he was twenty-two years old and nothing would happen."

"And?"

"Dead two weeks later, hit by a drunk driver." She set down the mug and scrubbed her face with her hands. "The worst part now? I'm receiving more and more frequent visions, and they're becoming more intense. I'm scared to touch anyone, which is kind of inconvenient if you consider my occupation. I'm the angel of death."

Her comment hit too close to the mark. What would Allie think when she learned the truth about him? And how screwed up had his world become, where the basis of his only human relationship in seventy years was pain? "Trust me, you're not. But why did you become an ER doctor?"

"Might as well bring relief to someone. At least in this job, I can prevent death, even bring people back from it."

"Even when you see visions of patients?"

"No. I try to save everyone, but when I get a vision, those patients always die. Maybe not in my ER, but after they transfer to another facility or after they get home." Her head came up with a snap. "So, can you make this stop?"

"I think so."

Her green eyes narrowed, as tiny glints of gold sparked. "How do you know about my … problem?"

"I told a knowledgeable friend what happened. When you touched me, I felt all my pain inside sucked out, and it felt like a huge weight had been lifted." He struggled to meet her accusing glare. "I also knew you had seen a lot about me, and I needed to figure out why and how. My friend Barnaby says you're a Ward."

"A what?"

"A Ward. It's a human who can see death. They're very rare."

"Lucky me." She snugged her arms around her bent knees once more. "Why can you tell what I saw then? Are you a Ward, too?"

"Nope."

Her breathing rate increased. "So are you … dead?" She uncurled her legs and scooted away from him.

That was the response he'd dreaded. "Not exactly."

"Human?"

"I'm somewhere in between."

"What does in between mean?" Fine lines formed between her delicate brows.

"Let's just say it's complicated."

The glow in her emerald eyes faded to a flat, ice-cold glare. "Try me."

"I can't explain it all. Not now. But it relates to the visions you saw."

"Did you kill those people?"

The snapshots of his life history would disgust even the strongest person. "Yes, those were images from some wars where I killed my enemies at the time."

"Did you only kill enemies?"

"I only killed bad people," he hedged.

"Did you feel guilty about it?"

"Every time."

"You must have been all over the world in a short period of time."

By her perplexed expression, she was trying to make sense of the faces and old uniforms in the vision. It was not good for her to think too hard about what she saw.

As she opened her mouth to ask another question, he interrupted her. "Do you want me to show you how to block your ability or not?"

When she leaned forward, the V of her scrub top emphasized the cleft between her breasts. *Focus on anything but* that, *dammit.*

She tapped her chin. "As much as I want to know, you're going to have to answer some more questions for me."

"Not now. Let me help you first."

"Okay, but I'm not done asking questions."

"Agreed." He indicated her head with his hand. "So … ?"

"Yes. Show me how to block these visions. I can't live like this."

He wanted to help her. But he also needed to connect with her again. Craved that contact. If it helped her, that was a bonus, as far as he was concerned.

"Since you can see visions of me, I'll start by trying to hide some of myself." At her curious expression, he shrugged. "Barnaby said it was like holding back a sneeze."

Her unexpected laugh bubbling up acted like a drug for his soul. He needed more.

Smiling, she asked, "And what do I need to do? Not sneeze, too?"

"Have you ever been in a stiff, awkward situation where you have to be super polite? Maybe you don't like the person you're sitting next to at a social activity?"

"Sure. When I'm at a hospital board function and they ask if there are any concerns. No one really wants my opinion. I keep that stuff to myself and make nice."

"It's kind of like that. You have to put up a strong emotional shield."

She nibbled her lower lip and frowned. "I understand the shield part. But do I walk around all day long with this ... shield ... in place? Sounds exhausting."

His heart pounded. Would this work? Or would he destroy her mind? "According to Barnaby, it gets easier with time."

"All right," she whispered.

Silence stretched out in the room, interrupted by her snoring dog.

He rubbed his jaw. "If you don't mind, let's give it a try. You have to let me come into contact with you."

Patting the cushion next to her, she said, "Let's try. What's the worst that can happen? I'll see a vision of you and death? Already did that."

He sat next to her, inches away, and inhaled her clean scent of fresh air and outdoors and life. Vibrant, she embodied everything he wasn't. A mixture of desire and protectiveness blended inside of him. Although she fascinated him, he didn't want to hurt her, like what nearly happened in the ER. Then again, he wanted that rush of power.

Be careful.

Her lips thinned. "So how ... how do we start?"

As he concentrated on her wide, trusting eyes, the whispering sense of her presence just beyond his range of hearing started up again. He wanted his mouth over the pulse that flitted beneath the smooth skin of her neck.

Focus, damn it.

He rubbed his jaw. "I think ... Let's you and I get kind of ... braced. You get your shield up, and I'll try ... not to sneeze."

She giggled.

Hell, this plan was ridiculous.

Then, with an air of concentration, her jaw set and her gaze turned to cold steel. A polite, blank expression settled on her features.

Turning fully toward him, she said, "I think I'm good."

He held out his hands, palms up. "Give me your hands."

She flickered a wide-eyed glance at him, then shifted back to the emotionless expression. With shaking fingers, she reached for him.

Chapter 7

The minute her hands contacted Peter's heated palms, Allison plunged into the vision. Even though she was ready for it, the howling intensity took her breath away. Yet this time, when the images washed over her, they didn't burn like they had previously. A buzzing tingle in her fingertips served as a constant reminder of the connection. She floated in a protective bubble as the visions swirled around her; the numerous voices blended into a deafening cacophony of sound then receded until all she could hear was a soft roar, like a constant, blowing wind.

Peter's strong, firm grip enveloped her shaking hands. He tightened and relaxed the pressure several times as if he was holding back, like a car revving with the brakes still on. The wind continued to roar, but she felt safe and protected.

His brown eyes had turned onyx-black, boring into her soul. She couldn't move. When she lost focus for a moment, the visions began to hurt, but she gritted her teeth and made her mental wall stronger.

Peter took a deep breath and held it for a second.

The burning receded once more and Allison relaxed her guard.

His lips moved, but no sound came out. Frowning, she strained to hear. Bit by bit, his voice penetrated the blended wind of voices. Like tuning into an AM radio station, she finally heard him.

In his static-laced voice, he asked, "Is this hurting you?"

She shook her head, optimism beginning to grow inside. *Maybe I will be free.*

Through their joined hands, his warmth flowed up her arms and into her chest. New emotions flowed into her mind—Peter's emotions. Concern for her safety and desire for her was paramount in his thoughts, but a mist cloaked a portion of his mind.

Could she truly be in his consciousness? What about that part she couldn't see? Was he hiding something? Curious, she probed into the unclear area of thoughts, separating out and clarifying the visions of him one by one.

The woman Allison had seen before … the lady's cute bobbed hairstyle flattened into a sweaty mat of hair on her forehead. The woman wasted away. Suffered.

Crushing sadness lanced through Allison's chest. When the woman opened her mouth to speak, only a stale, mechanical puff of air came out. The taste of bitter regret in Allison's mouth was tangy and sour. Her heart ached, poignant, painful, and empty.

Then a debonair man with shiny, curled, black hair appeared, dressed in fine, old clothing, velvet trimmed with lace, like something out of a French painting. His smile didn't reach his coal-black, frigid eyes. She—no, Peter—shook hands with the man. Searing heat scalded her palm pressed to the man's hand. Then the man grinned, a rictus of a smile twisting his thin mouth into a hole of hellish laughter.

She plunged into Peter's emotions, experiencing hope, despair, followed by emptiness. Then … war? She flinched at nearby explosions, her ears ringing.

An Asian soldier died by Peter's hands, her hands. The sudden, driving urge to vomit seized every muscle in her body as she sensed the give in a man's flesh when the knife penetrated the soldier's ribcage, blood erupting. Brief elation spiked through the knife and along her—no, Peter's—arm. Her heart swelled with his hope, then crumpled in despair.

A swarthy man in a headscarf with a wound in his chest fell lifeless to the ground, blood squirting in pulses from a shredded heart. Again, the ever-present knife plunged into the crater of the wound, severing bloody flesh. Once more, her heart soared with hope, expectation, and then squeezed hard as crushing despair washed through her veins.

Peter clamped down on her hands, wrenching her out of the visions. His detached voice cut through the roaring wind. "What are you doing?"

"I see … " she whispered. "I see … all of you … inside … " She dug her nails into his hands. Peter's eyes narrowed. His darkness became a heavy, black cloak that settled on her shoulders. She suddenly weighed a million pounds. Couldn't move. Didn't care.

Then the weight lifted and the power of their connection surged; mainlining coffee wouldn't feel this good. She had become part of his emotions. His heart soared with the lightness of breaking free from prison, but it was much more. Elation, like water springing up from a dry garden fountain, rose from inside of him, rushed through his warm palms, and flowed into her arms.

Then a hunger, a need, strange and overpowering, flowed through her hands.

She froze.

The hunger was for her.

Trapped physically and mentally within the connection, she couldn't move. The winds roared in her mind, battering the bubble of her oasis.

Peter paused an inch from her mouth and inhaled, closing his eyes.

Still joined to him, she experienced an echo of his pleasure, his blazing desire. With a shudder, he let go of her hands and kissed her.

The quick shift of contact stunned Allison as the voices silenced for a split second and then returned in a softer timbre. The tempest became background noise now as she focused on the present.

He brushed gentle kisses over her lips. His hands covered her face from jaw to cheekbones, and again Allison sensed his power held in check as he cradled her head in a firm frame. Peter pulled her long hair loose from the clip, burying one hand in the strands before returning his other hand to caress the side of her face.

The dull roar of the mental communion fused with a rising tide of desire deep inside her core. Where did his emotions stop and hers begin?

Who cared?

Needing more, she leaned forward, kissing him back. She grasped the short hair at the nape of his neck, pulling him closer.

Peter growled, his deep rumble raising goose bumps on her arms. The gentle but insistent pressure of his hands and lips plundered her in a sensual, relentless onslaught. He descended onto her open mouth, devouring her with his tongue. With his hands on the sides of her head, he pressed her back onto the couch cushion, nipping at her lips with his teeth.

When he sucked part of her lip into his mouth and laved it with his rough tongue, something suppressed and primal uncoiled.

She scraped her nails over his tight neck and muscled shoulders. With every advance she made, he took the kiss even deeper, filling her every pore with his heat.

Without losing contact with her mouth, he reached down and swung her legs onto the couch.

Ivy snorted and gave a *whuff*.

Now kneeling on all fours, Peter caged Allison in his embrace.

Her heart thudded a drumbeat as he slowly lowered himself, resting on his forearms positioned outside her shoulders. His corded legs locked onto either side of her hips.

She reached under his arms and around his muscled torso, tugging him flush against her as delicious, intense heat covered her from head to toe.

With a groan, he took the kiss deeper. The connected visions continued to churn, but they now played like background conversation.

All of her focus centered on his powerful limbs, which bracketed her body. She was trapped in the most delicious way. A wave of deeper desire flowed into her core, and heat bloomed low in her belly as he pressed his pelvis down onto hers.

When she looked into his puma-black eyes and licked her lips, he dove back down, capturing her mouth again, plunging his tongue deeper into her mouth, branding her body and soul with his heat.

He lifted her shoulders until her head fell back. At the nip of his teeth on the soft skin of her neck, Allison shifted her hips, restless, needing more.

Increasing growls, white-hot kisses, and pressure from his hips intertwined with the visions and the murmuring voices in their linked minds. She floated, disconnected from the Earth, held in exquisite stasis as she shivered beneath his lips on her neck. She ran her hands over his muscled arms, bound tight as he held his weight off of her.

When he returned to her mouth, she met him eagerly. Groaning, he slanted to another angle, holding her head steady. While he kissed her, he leaned to one side, sliding his hand down to her waist. His arm beneath the small of her back arched her to him.

Bursts of pleasure percolated through her core. She'd never been this close to a man before. After her boyfriend's death years ago, she'd never allowed herself any intimacy for fear of more visions. What in the world had she been missing all these years? As her libido erupted into flames beneath Peter's heated hands, Allison had the intense desire to make up for lost time. Now.

He tugged on the hem of her scrub top, exposing her sensitive skin. His fingers trailing over her abdomen made her shiver, but not with cold.

Ivy jumped up and ran to the door, barking.

Disoriented, as though she'd been plunged into frigid water, Allison clutched at Peter's shoulders.

His arms tightened, he shoved her shirt down, and covered her with his body.

She followed his scan of the room until it rested on the living room window, where a shadowed figure darted away.

Snarling a curse, Peter flew off of her and ran to the front door.

When she joined him, he grabbed her arm, yanking her behind him, his face contorted with fury. His back muscles bunched beneath her hands.

He reached for the door handle. "Stay inside."

Ivy jumped and spun in a circle next to them.

"Ivy! Sit." Allison pointed at the floor and her dog reluctantly obeyed. "What's going on?" she whispered. Her heart pounded and not just from fear.

He shushed her at the crunch of quick footsteps growing fainter on the gravel outside the house. "Please"—he pressed on her shoulders—"stay here."

He flung open the door and, faster than was humanly possible, sprinted down the driveway and onto the road.

Ivy's giant tail eagerly beat the floor, ready for more fun.

She stared at her dog. "The heck I'm staying inside."

Ivy gave a happy bark, ready for a new adventure. Allison snapped on Ivy's leash and the two of them jogged down the driveway, searching the area for anything abnormal. A cold chill shot down her spine. Who had been at her house? She'd always felt safe out here. Until now.

In the distance, a car engine revved and gravel scattered. As she turned down the long dirt lane that led from her house to the main road, she spied a figure at the end of the lane. Her heart thudded as she glanced over her shoulder. How quickly could she reach the house?

The figure jogged toward her, and her senses tingled. Ivy yipped, tail wagging.

Peter.

When he reached her, Peter came to a dead stop, his fists clenched, face red, rage oozing from every inch of him. "I told you to stay in the house," he said. He wasn't even out of breath.

"I had my security system with me." She motioned toward Ivy, who sat at Allison's side, her tail raising small puffs of dirt with each enthusiastic thump.

He looked up at the sky. "What would she do? Lick the intruder to death?"

"Hmmph. You'd be surprised at how Ivy takes care of me. She seems to know good people from bad."

"That won't keep you alive," he growled. "Let's get back to your house."

His grasp on her upper arm generated warmth deep in Allison's gut. Low-level images of the faces from Peter's mind intruded again, and she tamped them down exactly as he'd taught her. Her mind cleared enough to focus on the here and now. Funny, the blocking mechanism worked with less concentration this time. Was this skill universal or isolated to her connection with Peter?

"I have to find out who that guy was," he said.

"Did you see him?"

"No, he took off before I could see the license plate on the car, but I got a brief glimpse of the man. I wonder if he was a guy I saw around town the other day."

"How could you remember one person?"

"Well, I was looking—"

She yanked her arm away. "Looking?"

"I was just looking around." He didn't meet her gaze.

When they arrived back at her house, Peter tensed again as he scanned the area.

"What is it?" she asked as they approached the front window.

"See these footprints?"

"Kind of." She could barely make out the indentations.

"They belong to someone maybe around my size. But see how deep the impressions are? Solid guy. And I presume he's all muscle by the way he took off."

Allison shivered and rubbed her chilled arms.

He put his hand on her arm again. "Let's get you inside. It's cool out."

She spun away. "No. Peter, *what* are you?"

A muscle jumped in his jaw. "Can we talk inside?"

"No." She crossed her arms. Even Ivy sat down, refusing to budge.

Peter groaned.

"I'm not letting you back inside unless you tell me how you moved so quickly."

Hopefully he wouldn't call her bluff. With his bizarre strength and speed, he could get past her and into the house in two seconds flat if he so desired.

He sighed, running a hand through his dark brown hair. Still as a statue, he finally responded. "It might be easier if I showed you."

Her heart sped up as she gamely followed him to the edge of the woods near her house. Was this a colossal mistake? Ivy liked Peter, so that was something. Her dog had pretty good instincts. Hopefully, her own instincts were correct as well.

• • •

They reached a stand of pine trees behind Allie's house. One dead ponderosa pine had fallen and now leaned against the other trees. When Peter wrapped his arms around the trunk, his hands didn't quite meet. *Should be about right.*

Suddenly, he stopped, frozen in place by doubt. Should he proceed with this unnerving demonstration? Strange, he'd never been self-conscious before. Damn it, he wanted more of this woman. More of her light spirit, her soft and sexy kisses. This display had the potential to rip apart what fragile threads tied them together.

Could he lie to her?

Never.

Decision made.

"I've never shown anyone what I can do. So could you stand over there, away from this area?"

He indicated a spot midway between the copse of trees and her house, and Allie and Ivy moved away, neither taking their eyes off him.

Trapped again. Only now it was a freakish show-and-tell gone sideways. Barnaby had said to let the Ward know what he was, but this couldn't be the right thing to do, could it? Besides, Allie had managed fine without full disclosure up until now.

Well, hell. Let's get this damn circus over and be done with it.

He hauled the trunk out of the ground, breaking off thick roots in the process, and dropped the tree with a deafening crash. The sound reverberated in the cold morning air until dead silence remained.

Even Ivy's ever-moving tail stilled. Allie stood like a statue, her fair skin pallid. At least she remained standing.

Grimly, he returned to the bizarre exhibition.

Snapping off a sharp branch, he dashed over to Allie, all in the space of a millisecond. He presented his bare forearm and gouged a gash down his arm. When she gasped and stepped forward, he held up a hand. Like with all injuries, even though the wound hurt like hell, his skin began to knit back together after mere seconds. Her horrified green stare gutted him. But he wasn't done yet.

Sprinting back to the tree, he braced the middle portion of the trunk against a rock. Then he brought his foot down, shattering the trunk with an ear-splitting explosion. After repeating the action six feet up the tree, he'd freed up a good 400 pounds of trunk. Glancing again at Allie, her eyes like giant green saucers, he heaved the trunk to the other side of the clearing, a hundred yards away.

He took a few deep breaths and brushed off his hands.

Well, that's that. Indebted freak show over. Should be obvious I'm not human.

He turned around.

Allie was gone.

Chapter 8

Peter caught a flash of light blue fabric disappearing around the corner of the house, and he took off at a sprint, intercepting Allie at the front porch. She backed away, mouth agape. Her fear would've broken his heart, if he had one left.

"What the heck?" she said, flashing eyes that blamed him without saying a word.

He flinched away until his anger flared, fanned by the years of his own hatred. He didn't need to see the horror on her face to know what a monster he'd become. Damn it all, he'd put himself out there, trusted her, and showed her his abilities. Did he really expect her complete acceptance? How naïve could he be?

Her chest heaved. She breathed too quickly. "I trusted you! I let you in my house. You could've—"

When she lunged toward the door, he reached out to steady her.

She recoiled and cowered against the doorjamb.

Not for the first time in his miserable life, he hated who he was. The horror on her beautiful face, her eyebrows raised and tears shimmering, reminded him that he existed only to bring pain to others. His despair ballooned to ungodly proportions.

"I'm not going to hurt you." Should he touch her or keep his distance? Damn it, her suffering was his fault. His hands dropped.

She touched her lips. "Oh my gosh, you, we almost—" The moisture in her eyes shoved him back to reality.

He had to keep her safe. Forever.

What the hell? Where did "forever" come from? The realization blew him away. He needed her. Needed her to accept him. Needed her to … what? To hang out together? To date? Not until he accomplished the Meaningful Kill, and progress in that area didn't look promising. But if it meant a possible future with Allie, he'd redouble his efforts for the Meaningful Kill. If only he could figure out how.

"You have to believe me, Allie," he said. "I would never cause you harm. Nothing could ever make me hurt you."

When she shivered in the cool air, he fought the compulsion to wrap her in his arms and warm her body.

With a weak laugh, she said, "You know, the visions of death I got from you, they made sense in a weird way. Because of my gift, I accepted what I saw as par for my crazy life, you know? But seeing what you can actually *do* puts those images in a new light. I shouldn't have ever started this process with you today. It was a mistake." She took a shuddering breath. "Look, I know you're capable of doing whatever you want to do." Her expressive eyes pierced his soul. "But I'm asking you to leave."

With her back against the door, she stood up straight, so small and brave, even knowing what Peter could do.

Damn it, he could take anything he desired by sheer force. He could take her. But even when he was human, he had never imposed himself on any woman, and he sure wasn't about to start now.

He scrubbed at his jaw and backed away, one step, then another. Leaving her here was the hardest thing he'd done in a long time. The physical distance between them created a strange vacuum in his chest, an echo that kept trying to reach out to connect, even as the distance increased.

Ivy whined and put her head on Allie's hip.

Allie grasped the front door handle, not taking her eyes off him. Maybe she thought being in the house would protect her from something like him. Hell, he could rip the door off the hinges with one hand. Despite every fiber of his being screaming at him to go after her, he would not intrude.

He loathed the terror in her eyes.

Waving Ivy into the house, she stood stiffly at the half-opened door. "Thank you for helping me block all this." She waved toward her head. "And for trying to find whoever was outside my house. Thank you."

"Allie, I swear I'll never harm you. You have to believe me."

Her shoulders slumped as her knuckles whitened on the edge of the door.

He nearly lost his resolve to give her space. "I want you safe. That's a promise."

Without saying a word, she closed the door with a click, followed by the dull clunk of the deadbolt.

Maybe he'd made a mistake in showing her how to block the visions. What if the big boss found out? What would happen to a mortal who knew about their kind? Barnaby's friend, Susan, knew years ago and she survived. Was it because they hadn't told anyone? Peter's head spun. He had to keep Allie safe until he figured out what to do, and before an innocent got hurt.

Collateral damage was not an option.

Regrets aside, deep down, he'd help her all over again, even if it led to this same rejection. Her soft lips haunted him, and he could feel her smooth skin beneath his fingers, smell her scent of fresh, mountain air. Even now, he had a faint connection to her, filled with anguish that, of course, was his fault.

Peter went wherever death was required, wherever his assignments mandated. This gentle woman had complicated his assignment. On top of discovering and killing his target, he now needed to keep Allie safe from whatever had been lurking outside her house.

Hell.

His cell phone rang, jarring him as he got into his truck. He groaned when he saw the number.

"Dante."

He turned the ignition and backed out of Allie's driveway.

"How's it going in La Grind?"

The only thing Dante liked more than killing and sex was bad puns. "Not that great, thanks for asking. Why're you calling?"

"Can't a guy call and check on his brother?"

Peter turned onto the country road and headed back to La Grande. "Sure, but I'm not your brother and you never call to check on me."

"Just seeing how you and that pretty doctor are doing."

"We're not. I'm trying to finish this assignment."

"Don't believe you. I can hear it in your voice, bro."

Hearing a three-time centenarian like Dante use slang always made Peter grin. The 1960s had been particularly frustrating, as Dante's vocabulary had relied heavily on colloquialisms such as "groovy" and "far out," warped at times by his friend's Swedish accent.

But it damn sure wasn't funny enough to continue with this conversation. It was time to bring up Dante's favorite topic: Dante.

"How'd your assignment in Boise go? Did you get some action while you were there?"

"Of course, bro, of course. I made some hotties' nights, over and over. And finished my assignment … or your old assignment."

"No release from your contract?"

A pause. "No, it must not have been the Meaningful Kill I needed." The normally talkative Dante fell silent.

"Dante? Can I ask you a question?"

"Shoot."

"You ever hate who you are?"

"You kidding? I'm the happiest 300-year-old Swedish national the world has ever known. It doesn't appear I'm going to die anytime soon, and I'm seeing all of history unfold in front of me."

"What about growing old with someone? Do you ever wonder how that would be?"

"You going soft on me, bro? I'm not settling down. It's overrated. I need to keep my options open. Hey, you been talking with Barnaby or something?"

"How did you know?"

"Good guess. He's like a celebrity. Hell, he was a few hundred years older than me when he finished his contract. When was he born? Fifteen hundreds or something like that? Even brushed shoulders with Queen Elizabeth, the old-old one, not the recent old one."

Peter pulled his truck into the hotel parking lot. "Barnaby knows a lot of stuff. His wife died a while back, didn't she?"

"Yep. He's getting old, too. Like human old."

Once, years ago, Peter had dreamed of growing old with Claire. She had died in her eighties, with her loving family surrounding her—loving family that didn't include Peter. Once he'd sacrificed his mortality for her, though, the rules prevented him from being part of her life ever again. His dreams of a life together with Claire got sucked down the drain, along with what remained of his cursed soul. All that he got in return was forever. Forever Indebted. Forever a killer. Forever a prisoner. "Must be odd to live all of those centuries and then experience a normal life and death."

Dante snorted. "Dude, you have gotten philosophical. Why don't I come up there and keep you company?"

"No!" The last thing he needed was for Dante to wreak havoc on the good people of this town while Peter tried to figure out what to do about Allie.

"Yeah, but I'm bored."

"Go read a book or something." Peter rolled his eyes.

"I've read them all."

"Have a good day, Dante."

"You too, Petey. See you soon."

As Peter protested, the line went dead. He groaned. He'd have to babysit Dante to keep the big Swede from running amok in this nice town, enjoying one of his drunk orgies. The innocent citizens would never know what hit them.

Chapter 9

Allison spent the next two days alone. A glass of wine to calm her racing thoughts didn't work. Reading novels didn't work. An Internet search about Wards didn't work. As a matter of fact, the Internet only made passing mention of Wards, with no definitive information. In this day and age she should've been able to find something, some primary source description, some reference, but her search turned up nothing.

At least she had the potential to "turn off" her visions. If she could prepare properly, she wanted to try to block Sarah and Quincy. The mere possibility of having a vision of someone else she loved made her blood run cold.

What about Peter? She touched her lips. She still felt him there, surrounded by his masculine scent, felt his rough hands roving over her arms and face. And what about his demonstration of freakish strength and speed? The sound of that entire trunk shattering sent chills down her spine, even now. If he could do that to a tree, what hope did she have if he turned that force on her or anyone else?

So what did she know about him now? Not a whole lot more than when they first met. She knew what he could *do*, but not what he *was*. She could guess that he wasn't exactly human, but how? Why? She shivered. Was he dangerous?

Of course he was dangerous.

She had witnessed his skills. She knew about him. Would he return to silence her?

For the love of all that was holy, she had lived in fear of visions of other family members for much too long. She'd used her career to level the cosmic playing field—the lives saved by her medical skills made up for the inevitable lives lost from each vision. Never in her wildest dreams had she considered the possibility of a normal, intimate relationship. And damn it all, but for a brief moment, she'd had the keys to the kingdom within her grasp. Peter had unlocked feelings she'd never experienced before; he had awakened the real woman inside of Allison.

But as soon as her silly pipe dream of companionship came within her reach?

Her potential suitor ripped a tree out of the ground. With his bare hands.

Typical. She should've known better by now. In her warped life, hope always ended in pain.

When she took Ivy out for brief, necessary walks, that crawly sensation crept up the back of her neck. Was it her imagination or something truly outside? Or another aspect of that strange sense of Peter echoing faintly in her mind?

The curtains in her house remained shut. She missed the sun, but the memory of the man through the front window overrode her desire for a light and airy home.

At night she woke up in a sweaty panic, time and again. Seven a.m. came much too early, and she had to move it to make it to the hospital on time. She had planned to take a week off after her next twenty-four-hour shift.

God, she would go stir crazy.

During her shift, every time the ER doors whooshed opened, her heart thudded. Male staff and patient voices in a certain timbre tightened her neck muscles until she could no longer relax. A perverse part of her longed to see Peter again. Even with his supernatural strength and speed, she longed for those strong arms to wrap around her, those firm lips to explore her body.

To distract her from memories of his body, she left her gloves off for routine exams and tried blocking the patients' visions, a skill that thankfully required all of her concentration. No images of death intruded, but then again, her gift had always occurred at random intervals. But her ability had changed. When she touched people, even if there was no sense of a vision, something still held her back, like a piece of cellophane between her hand and the patients' skin.

Another discovery occurred in the wee hours of her shift. As her fatigue grew, it took extreme effort to maintain the blocking ability. Unable to hold up the block, her control slipped at two in the morning and she endured an excruciating image of impending death for a gentleman having chest pain. They had flown the man out to Portland with an acute heart attack. A few hours later, she learned that he had indeed died. Of course he did. Maybe her skill would improve with practice or rest. If only she could get to that point where she no longer saw the death of others, it would be worth it.

When her shift ended Saturday morning, she headed home for a quick run, avoiding the wooded trails. After a shower, she was tired but ready for the day. Eyeing the light clouds, Allison grabbed a fleece and threw it on over her long-sleeved T-shirt and jeans, now eager to cheer on Quincy in the season-opener soccer jamboree. Marcie, who played an Internet-based meteorologist when she wasn't the ER receptionist, had said there was a good chance of snow tomorrow and Monday, but the early spring weather should stay decent for today.

Near the soccer fields at the university, masses of brightly uniformed five- to eleven-year-olds teemed with unbridled energy. A bittersweet smile crossed her lips. None of these children would ever be hers.

Allison clipped on Ivy's leash to allow her dog to trot next to her. When she reached the field for five- and six-year olds, she spotted Sarah and her husband, Bryce. Allison had immediately liked her brother-in-law when she met him years ago, not only because he adored her sister, but because he was just a good, normal guy. She should try finding one of those someday.

Actually, she had accomplished this task. She'd gone and found herself a nice guy. Damn it all, he wasn't just nice, he was sexy. In his arms, she had come to life. In his arms, she had finally felt safe.

The only problem? He was not exactly human. A minor detail marring her otherwise idyllic life inconveniently riddled with death and the inability to get close to anyone. What a colossal freaking joke.

No. She was not going to wallow in self-pity. Not today. She exhaled, rolling her shoulders to work out the knots that had been building.

As she waded through the scrum of kids clad in neon orange Ivy was showered with kisses and pats, much to her hedonistic dog's delight.

The coach's game plan was no match for the kids' exuberance. The whistle blew, and all semblance of organization ceased as every child on the field converged on the ball. Well, every child except for Quincy standing off in the far corner, alternately picking clovers and waving at her parents and Allison.

"It's always a mess." Bryce cringed and waved back.

Quincy had a close call, almost kicking the ball. Allison cheered wildly and grinned, a foreign sensation that relaxed her tense facial muscles.

Sarah sighed. "The best part of the day is snacks after each game. The sheer quantity of orange wedges and Gatorade should have her bouncing off the walls all night long." She batted her eyelashes at Bryce.

He pulled at his brown goatee. "No way. She's your kid today. I had to play fairy princess last weekend with her. I had to wear a tiara," he added in a horrified whisper hidden behind one hand for Allison.

Then a parent approached him and asked about the status of keeping vagrants off Main Street. Bryce shifted gears from doting dad to police chief as he answered the woman's questions in a professional, concerned manner.

Allison nudged her sister. "He's always on the clock, huh?"

"Mmm-hmm. He wants to do a good job, and I'm used to disruptions. Personally, I think he likes the notoriety. Well, you would know. I'm surprised no one's hit you up for medical advice yet."

"The day's young."

After the first game, Quincy ran over and petted Ivy, setting the dog's tail into lethally rapid motion. "Did you see me?" she asked.

"Oh, you did great!" Allison said. "Boy, you were all over that field!"

Sarah rolled her eyes, handed Quincy a sports bottle, and patted her on the shoulder. "Rest up, you've got two more games today."

Apparently satisfied, Quincy rejoined her teammates and received further instructions from the patient coach.

With Bryce occupied, this was a perfect time for some girl talk. "Can I ask you a big favor?"

"Sure. You want to babysit Quincy for a month?"

"That whirling dervish? She's all yours. No, I had a serious question to ask you."

"Shoot." Sarah smiled.

Suddenly chilled, Allison rubbed her arms. "Something has changed in my visions. I think I can do more."

Sarah gasped. "What do you mean, more? You're having more of them, right?"

"Yes, but that used to be the only thing I could do. Now I think I can do more."

"Like what?"

Allison stared at the turf, hoping to hide the warmth creeping into her face. "Well, I went into Peter's mind the other day."

"Explain. Now."

Sarah responded without question; quite the commentary on the sad state of Allison's life, that something this strange seemed so normal. Briefly, she described the recent encounter with Peter, minus the passionate kisses that nearly led to more and the bizarre demonstration of his strength.

She caught herself touching her lips and shoved her hand into a jeans pocket. "So when I came into contact with Peter, I saw the death visions, like I always do. But then my ability went into another gear I didn't know I had. I slipped into his mind, dug around, and pulled out his memories and thoughts. Sounds insane, doesn't it?"

Sarah tugged at her shoulder-length hair. "With you, anything is possible. Are you sure you weren't imagining things? Or maybe there's something weird about him that made you see things. You did say the first time you met him, it was strange."

Allison shifted from one foot to another. "That's right. That's why I wanted to see if you'd let me try. Um, on you."

Her sister stood still for a full minute. Just as Allison was going to retract the request, Sarah nodded.

"Go for it."

"You're sure?"

"If your power is changing, you need to understand it. I'm a good guinea pig. There's not much you don't know about me. Besides, I'm not scared of my little sister's ESP."

"What about surprise side effects? Anything could happen."

"It'll be fine."

"Wow. Thank you."

Her sister's thin, pressed lips turned up at the corners. "So, you want to do it right here?"

"Now?"

"No better time than the present. No one's paying attention to us. It'll look like we're two sisters chatting. Which we will be. Mentally."

Allison's breath came too fast. "Until your head explodes."

"No talk like that. I'll be fine."

"Yes, but I don't trust myself."

"I do. So give it a whirl, sis. What do you need me to do?"

"I'm not sure. All I know is that there has to be physical contact."

"All righty, then. Come on in."

Sarah faced the soccer game, inclined her head toward Allison, and grasped her hand.

The sensation developed differently than with Peter, but there was no death to see, thank God. Allison let down her guard and slid into her sister's mind. Bright, happy light surrounded her. And why shouldn't there be light? This was Sarah. Of course her sister's positive qualities went all the way to her core being. Allison pushed aside the mental curtains in Sarah's mind like shimmering gossamer. With her virtual self, Allison probed around, not sure what she was looking for but trying to be gentle about it. The last thing she wanted to do was hurt Sarah.

The wind sensation surrounded Allison, like with Peter, but it felt smoother, softer. It didn't batter her this time.

Peripherally, she became aware of Sarah's firm grip through their joined hands, but no pain exploded with the contact. How strange. The death visions always came with discomfort, but this was a warm and curious sensation. Maybe because there was no death visible, the vision didn't hurt.

Allison dove deeper, pushing through the diaphanous layers. A particular bright light formed into Quincy as a baby, and a warm, hopeful glow of new motherhood expanded in Allison's chest. A lump formed in her throat.

Digging deeper, she caught a glimpse of a younger Bryce. Allison shouldn't be seeing such passion and love in his eyes. That gaze was meant for her sister, but Allison gained all of her perspective. Brief jealousy twisted the image into something ugly until she took a deep breath in and out.

Another layer deeper, she struggled to move the heavier curtain, but she finally succeeded. There was her mother, curled up on the carpet after a bender, sweaty and moaning. Sharp sadness stabbed Allison in the heart. It was her fault that Mom suffered; it was her visions that pushed Mom over the edge.

Go deeper, Sarah's whispered voice drifted through the sound of rushing air.

I don't want to see.

You need to.

The curtains she moved for the last layer were heavy lead. There he was. But her father's withered body did not appear, dissolving beneath the chemotherapy, as Allison had remembered him.

Instead, the image Sarah kept locked deep in her memory was simple and stunning.

They were all having a picnic together, the last day together as a normal family. Allison, Sarah, Mom, and Dad. Before the visions started. Before everything changed.

Allison hadn't noticed the glances her parents gave each other, the way her mother's eyelashes batted or how her father quirked an eyebrow and winked. But this was Sarah's memory. Their parents twined normal, healthy hands together. Mom rested her head on Dad's shoulder and sighed. When ants threatened the basket of food, Dad jumped up and swatted the intruders off the blanket, grinning the whole time.

The smell of grass and soil slid into Allison's mind. She and Sarah had rolled down the little hill over and over again, their girlish knees and hips tumbling until neither of them could walk in a straight line. They had collapsed in laughter, surrounded by the leaves shushing in the wind and insects buzzing nearby. Above them, on the hillside, Mom's and Dad's faces shone.

The memory of the last perfect day that marked the end of a perfect life.

Enough. Quit wishing for the past. For what she could never have.

Pulling back out of her sister's mind, Allison squinted in the bright sunlight. The pleasant cacophony of scurrying kids eventually brought her back to the here and now. She let go of Sarah's hand.

"Are you okay?" she asked.

Her sister's eyes shone with tears.

More pain. The theme of Allison's life. "Oh God, I'm so sorry, I'll never do that again."

"No, it's okay, Al. Some of those images were beautiful. I had buried those memories."

"I didn't hurt you?"

"Not at all. It was weird. I knew you were there, but then pictures, flashes of memories, appeared like I'd thought of them myself. That's really cool."

Allison cringed at the pain lancing through her forehead. "I don't know if 'cool' is the right term. Hey, do you feel a sense of me now?"

"Like in my head?"

"Yes. I still get a little whispering sense of you in my own mind. Can you feel me there?"

Sarah frowned. "No, nothing at all; it's like nothing happened. Is that normal?"

Allison shrugged and stuffed her hands in her pockets. "Who knows?"

"Wow, your power really has changed. Who would've thought? A brand new ability. Good for you."

"I don't know about it being good, but thanks for letting me experiment on you." Allison threw her arms around her sister's neck, then stepped back, blinking away her burning tears. They stood in silence while the soccer game continued.

A new tingle began on the back of Allison's neck and crept up into her scalp, bringing her head up to scan the area.

A man in a leather jacket stood in the next field over. His crew cut and gaunt jawline gave him a severe appearance, even at a distance, but he seemed bulky beneath the jacket. He had some tics, too, repetitively touching his ears and the back of his head. The man couldn't hold still, and he wasn't watching the games. He seemed to be searching the sidelines and talking to himself. Maybe he had some mental illness. Hard to tell at this distance.

The tingle continued but had an uncomfortable edge to it, unlike the mental echoes from Peter and Sarah. She rubbed the nape of her neck as breathing became difficult.

The recent connection with Sarah must have put Allison's nerves on edge. Too warm, Allison shrugged out of the fleece and laid it on a nearby camp chair.

Focusing on the game, she forced a smile over her lips and took a few slow, cleansing breaths. Better.

When she glanced toward the other field, there was no sign of the man. Probably nothing but her hyperactive imagination, revved up from the experiment with her new powers. She pushed the last vestiges of unease to the side and refused to consider anything except enjoying the rest of the lovely day with her family.

Chapter 10

Peter had driven around La Grande for several days, hunting the man from Allie's house. The guy must have gone to ground. Maybe he left town, although that answer in no way satisfied Peter.

Focusing on the search was like walking through sludge. He literally couldn't get Allie out of his head. The memory of her sweet lips, her scent, her soft body in his arms superimposed itself on everything he saw. He had to use his time searching for the stalker, although he would much rather spend the time with Allie. All he wanted was to possess Allie's body and mind again and let the soothing connection assuage the evil he had become. The impulse horrified him. He'd never been on the verge of losing control, or at least not this close to the edge.

Beyond the distracting memory of her soft, sexy body, that mental connection continued, buzzing in the background of his thoughts. Did she have a similar feeling? He hadn't had time to ask there on her porch. Claire had once looked at him with horror and fear like that. At least with Claire, his sacrifice made up for her rejection.

Being around Allie was different. Claire had been a sweet and loving wife, but Peter had been more of a father figure to his young bride. Allie possessed a unique strength of character, no less sweet but a contrasting quality. Like fine champagne, he craved more of her effervescence.

He scrubbed at his jaw. Damn it, he needed to look for the stalker, not moon over a woman.

Driving through the Eastern Oregon University campus, he slowed down to avoid the children running around. A "Soccer Jamboree" sign flapped in the early spring breeze. Mindful of the kids, he traveled down the street until a familiar green Subaru

Outback caught his attention. Parking nearby, he joined the spectators at the fields.

The tree-lined street afforded some cover as he peered from behind his sunglasses into the crowd. When he spotted Allie at the end of one field, her hips encased perfectly in form-fitting jeans, his gut clenched. The long-sleeved T-shirt might've hidden her curves, but he knew better. His fingers spread out, recalling how her skin flowed under his hands. She stood next to the woman he'd seen the other day in the ER. He allowed himself a tight smile at their spirited cheering for an orange-uniformed girl waving to them—the princess from the ER.

Positioned far enough away that he wouldn't be recognized, Peter remained close enough to observe. When the young girl ran up to hug her parents and Allie and then skipped back to the game, jealousy tightened its fist around his throat until he couldn't swallow. His was a pathetic existence devoid of anything real or good. So what emotions remained? Bitterness and lust.

Outstanding.

He studied the field and street. On the next field over, a man stood off by himself, adjusting his jacket over thick shoulders and looking around with wide eyes. Only he wasn't watching the game. Peter traced the direction of the man's gaze.

Allie.

Peter's spine went ramrod stiff.

His fists clenched.

Hell. The man in the leather jacket stared intently at her. Was this the guy outside her house? Peter grabbed the tree until bark shredded beneath his fingers as he kept the man in his sights. He wanted to race over and make the man stop … stop what? Watching a game? Watching spectators? Maybe Peter's overprotective instincts blinded him to normal life. There was no way to prove that man did anything wrong. Peter would have to continue to observe.

After the game ended, the little girl ran over for an exuberant recap, judging by the clapping, high fives, and hugs all around. Searing acid boiled in his stomach. Family. Love. Two things he could never have.

Allie handed Ivy's leash to the other woman and strode toward the sports complex's bathroom near the road. Slinking behind a tree, Peter peered around. The bounce in Allie's step radiated life and energy. The wiggle in her backside evoked more carnal feelings in him.

With effort, Peter dragged his eyes away from Allie's trim form. Where was the man in the leather jacket? He searched again.

Right as Allie turned onto a concrete hallway between the restrooms, Peter caught a glimpse of the man dodging around the opposite side. Instincts screaming an alarm, Peter took off at his quickest human walk, trying not to draw attention but wanting to move faster.

Allie's pain exploded inside his mind, staggering him forward two steps.

Her scream reverberated inside his head, turning his blood to ice.

No longer caring if anyone saw him, Peter covered the distance in mere seconds. As he skidded around the corner, Allie cried out, her shriek muffled by the cinderblock walls and cheering crowds nearby. His vision went red, and he heard only a howl of air in his ears.

The stocky man with the buzz cut gripped Allie's hand in what would appear to an observer as an amiable handshake, but her pain echoed through the mental connection, staggering Peter backwards a few steps. Stark, desperate terror clear in her wide eyes, Allie pulled at her hand, but it remained trapped in the man's grip. Her pupils constricted. Swirls of gold in her green, bulging eyes redefined horror as she gasped for air with a strangled gurgle.

The man shot Peter a nasty grin, and his thin lips curled in feral pleasure. "She's interesting, this innocent. She'll be a tasty, tasty treat. Yummy, yummy, yummy." Spittle formed at the corners of his snarling mouth as the man pulled her toward him, his tongue darting out.

Peter couldn't think straight over the roar of rage in his mind. "Get away from her!"

He leapt.

The man sneered and shoved Allie forward. She would have hit her head on the concrete if Peter hadn't grabbed her shoulders to slow her fall. Tight wheezes escaped past pursed lips as she crumpled forward onto hands and knees. When Peter looked up again, there was no trace of the gaunt-faced man. Torn, he fought between his impulse to run after the man and kill him and the instinct to help Allie.

"Allie?" He eased her into a sitting position in the open walkway. She sagged against the rough wall.

Her choked sob tore him in two.

Peter ran his hands over her, searching for injuries. "What did he do to you? Are you hurt?"

Her skin was the color of paper ash. She recoiled until she finally focused on him. "I'm going to be sick." Struggling to her feet, she staggered into the women's bathroom.

Peter helped her into a stall, supporting her as she knelt and vomited, her lithe frame shaking. He brushed her long hair back and handed her a paper towel to wipe her face.

He would kill that man for touching her.

When she flinched, he relaxed the grip pinching her shoulder, the grip he wished were around that man's neck.

After her breathing calmed, he helped her stand and they stepped out of the stall. A woman entering the bathroom sniffed as the corner of her mouth turned down.

Allie whispered, "You can go out. I'll be right there. I'm okay." Her hoarse voice stopped him dead in his tracks.

"Your voice. Are you all right?"

When she coughed, the harsh, dry sound raked across his nerves. "Couldn't breathe for a second there, but I'm better now, thanks." She inclined her head toward the woman in the stall and raised her fine eyebrows.

Peter backed out of the restroom and paced outside until Allie exited. When she finally emerged, the haunted, hollow expression in her dull eyes made him reel back a step. He supported her upper arms as she leaned against the cold cinderblock wall.

"What the heck? Who was that man?" she asked, her sweet voice still raw, her green gaze drilling into his.

His thundering heart injected hot rage through his veins. The need to hunt the cretin who had hurt her began to overwhelm the need to remain close to Allie.

He rocked back on his heels. "I've never seen him before." He paused. "Strike that. I saw him around town the other day. I bet that's the guy from outside your house."

"What?" she whispered.

He held her upright as she staggered forward, her ashen face contorted. When she clutched at her midsection, he drew her up into his arms. *Protect her.* He wrapped one arm around her lower back and covered her head beneath his other hand, tucking her into his chest, wanting to surround her with his body.

When she trembled, he tried to let go, worried that their physical contact might trigger a vision. With a sob, she fisted her hands in the material of his shirt. Damn it. If she needed him, he would hold on to her as long as she wanted. Taking a deep breath and concentrating, he blocked his mind from her. He could at least protect her from the painful images of his kills.

She straightened up and leaned back. "Oh God, he was near my house."

"I presume that's who he was. I can't be completely sure." He held her secure in his arms. "Allie, can we sit down? You don't look so good."

He kept her close until they reached a street-facing park bench. Peter stood over her, scanning the area as Allie leaned forward, put her head in her hands, and took a few deep draws of air. He laid a hand on her upper back and rubbed lightly, taking care not to touch any skin.

After some minutes, she composed herself and stared bleakly at him, her eyes red-rimmed. The torment etched on her haggard features scored his heart.

He sat down, draping his arm behind her on the bench. "Can you tell me what happened?"

"The man triggered another vision." She frowned at her right hand and shook it vigorously. "I wasn't expecting it, couldn't block it. I tried, but the images came too fast, too hard."

He squeezed her shoulder through the T-shirt fabric. "What did you see?"

"This guy made your visions seem like preschool playtime. If I saw this guy killing people, then all I can say is that he obviously *liked* it."

"What?"

"They were bizarre images: a shoe, a lake, a child's bloody hands. And in some of the images, I saw him torture people. I heard—no, I actually felt the screams, the pain. Men, women … children. They were in agony. I can't even describe it all … " Her hair fell forward as she bowed her head again.

He reached for her, but closed his hand in a fist. "Is it okay if I touch you?"

She sniffed. "You won't hurt me. I've got you blocked. Strange, but it seems easier to do with you right now."

Peter pushed a lock of light brown hair back as glints of gold reflected in the sunlight. When he touched the soft skin on her cheek, there was only a little sense of connection. Maybe he was getting better at suppressing the memories, or she had become accustomed to his mental presence. He cleared his throat. "How did you get that much information from him? He made contact with you for only a few seconds."

"I don't know. All the images were instantly in my head. And I can still sense him in my mind. Like a bad aftertaste."

She shuddered again. Peter tightened his arm around her shoulders and tucked her into his side, where they sat silently.

To any casual observer, they appeared to be a couple simply relaxing on a park bench, enjoying an early spring day, but he knew better. Today, he had failed to protect her. He wouldn't make that same mistake again.

A balding man with a goatee whom Peter recognized as the young soccer player's father strolled over to their bench. "Al?"

"Hi, Bryce." She popped on sunglasses.

Peter wasn't buying her too-bright tone of voice.

"Are you okay?" Bryce eyed him suspiciously.

Peter kept his arm firmly around her shoulders. "She got sick, and … "

Allie jumped up from the bench with a quick, thin smile. "Bryce, Peter Blackstone. Peter, Bryce Zachary, my brother-in-law."

When the two men shook hands, Peter gave him a little more pressure than he should have.

"You, uh, from around here?" Bryce asked.

Think.

"I had planned to interview for a teaching position at the university when I got into a bad accident." He motioned toward Allie. "Doctor Al here patched me up, good as new." He grinned in what he hoped was a disarming expression. Smiling felt unnatural these days.

Bryce crossed his arms over his chest. "So what department at the school?"

"History. I'm a big World War II buff."

He uncrossed his arms. "Well, you escaped a close call then."

"Pardon?" Peter blinked.

"The accident. You're the guy who crashed off the interstate and down the embankment last week, right?" Bryce whistled. "You are one lucky guy, walking around healthy and all. Most folks wouldn't have survived that bad of an accident, much less feel fine a week later."

Peter smiled. "I had an excellent ER physician. And yes, very good luck."

"You need a ride home or something?" Bryce asked Allie.

"And miss the rest of Quincy's season debut? No way." Taking a few steps toward the field, she added, "They're getting ready to start the last game. We'd better get back before she thinks we've forgotten her."

As the kids lined up on the sideline, Bryce turned toward the restrooms. "I'll meet you back there in a minute."

After Bryce left, Peter stared down at her. "You sure you're all right?"

"Better now, thanks."

"I'm not sure I believe you." He placed one finger beneath her chin, appreciating the warmth of her skin and the low-level connection buzz that flowed between them. "So. Can I watch the game with you for a while?"

"So you can keep an eye out for that creep?"

"That's one reason. But the bonus is spending more time with you."

Color crept into her cheeks, making him smile. When she breathed deeply, he stared at her T-shirt for a moment too long. His pulse jumped.

She cleared her throat. "Come over and cheer on the Antelopes for a while."

"Antelopes? They're more like neon Oompa Loompas to me."

"You're probably more accurate."

As they turned to walk down to the field, a whiff of rotten eggs drifted by his nose.

He froze. *Hell.*

Sirens going off in his head, he searched the area. If his hunch was correct, Allie's life was at immediate risk, worse than from the man who had put his hands on her. Peter had to get her out of here.

"Would you excuse me a moment? I need to take care of something. I'll meet you at the field in a few minutes."

"Of course. Is there something I can do?"

He pretended to be calm. Anything to get her away from him. "No, please go to the field and stay with your family."

"Is there something wrong?" A line formed between her eyebrows.

"Not at all," he lied. "I'll be over in a moment."

After he'd reassured himself that she returned to the sideline with her sister, Peter slowly turned in a full circle. There, between two SUVs, a thin man preened in a side mirror. Peter couldn't miss the sheen of oil on the man's long, black, curled hair.

Damn, the knife on Peter's leg fired up, too, as it recognized its maker.

Jerahmeel looked up from his unabashed perusal and crooked a finger at Peter. He wore a deep purple suit with a maroon ruffle visible from his neck to his chest, a bizarre intersection of forty-years-late style and a garish interpretation of French Revolution chic. However, true to form, not a thread was out of place.

Peter's heart beat a tattoo against his chest wall as he approached his boss. Jerahmeel rarely appeared in person because it sapped too much of his energy. That's why he sent minions. So why had he taken the effort to show up now?

"Yes, my lord Jerahmeel. What may I do for you? Why are you here?" He swept his arm around to casually encompass the mundane human activities taking place in the park.

Jerahmeel's snicker grated like chalk on a board. "Checking in on your assignment." His thin red lips twisted into a moue of unhappiness. "You don't seem focused on your work."

"Of course I am, my lord." Peter ground his teeth.

"Tell me about that lovely *mademoiselle* you are courting."

"We aren't courting. She helped me after a bad accident, that's all. She's of no consequence."

Nothing good would come of his boss focusing his attention on Allie. Nothing.

Jerahmeel leaned close and inhaled deeply. "Ah, *parfum de femme*. She smells delicious. Who does she remind me of? Silly memory, I'll think of it soon."

Maybe Jerahmeel had distracted himself. Peter stood completely still, not breaking the silence. Somehow, he managed not to curl his lip while the sulfur-scented manifestation of Satan groomed himself to purulent perfection. When Jerahmeel finally raised his head to stare at Peter, those coal black eyes were cold and blank.

"You will not allow a *fille* to distract from the task I've set before you."

Peter locked his legs. "My focus on my work has never been in question."

Jerahmeel scowled as faint smoke rose from his head.

Hell.

Peter struggled to stay civil. All he wanted to do was run to Allie and act as a physical shield against this evil creature. "Actually, my lord, I don't know specifically what my assignment is. Would you illuminate me?"

"That's part of the fun, isn't it? Normally the assignment is clear. But I'm bored. I want to see if you can figure out your mission on your own." He licked his pinkie finger with the tip of his too-red tongue and smoothed a black eyebrow.

"I don't understand."

"I know you don't." Smoke coiled from a finger. His eyes glinted like two red embers in the depths of that unnatural stare. "See, you aren't focused enough. So know this—if you continue to pursue your interest in this mortal woman, I will ensure that she is destroyed. To keep you on track, of course."

Ice flooded Peter's veins—sweet Allie subjected to Jerahmeel's cruelty? "Hold on, there. You're not allowed to touch a mortal."

"I don't have to. There are other means of facilitating change." A tiny flame emanated from his middle fingertip. "You understand?"

"Of course. But I also know there are certain rules that bind you from intervening in humans' lives."

"*Merde.* How do you know this?"

Keep him from thinking about Allie. "I have well-informed friends."

"Well, I, too, have well-informed associates, Mr. Blackstone, and they are not bound as I am to silly rules."

Those silly rules were all that kept innocent humans from being mere nutrition for Jerahmeel. If he skirted the rules on technicalities, all humans were in danger.

Peter squeezed his hand into a fist. Even though his strength would be no match against something like Jerahmeel, Peter would die trying to keep his boss away from Allie. "You will not touch her."

"I will not have to." Jerahmeel blew out the flame and straightened his suit jacket before waggling his fingers. "Good day." In a blink and a whiff of sulfur, he was gone.

Allie had been marked. The attack by the man earlier this afternoon had to be connected. Maybe a precursor. Damn.

Peter might not be worthy of a future with Allie, but he could at least ensure that she lived to have a future of her own. Putting on what he hoped was a carefree—or at least concern-free—expression, he headed to the soccer field.

Chapter 11

Allison tried to clear away the hideous images, chafing her arms as though that nasty stalker had covered her in slime. Her life had flipped upside-down. Not only was she fighting a bizarre attraction to an even more bizarre unhuman, but now she had to worry about a crazy man who killed women and children attacking her again. How was that evil man connected to Peter? She experienced similar visions with both men. That resemblance couldn't be coincidence.

She wanted to ask Peter, but he was useless at the moment, locked in intense conversation with Bryce. Peter had casually mentioned playing football at Ohio State, and now thirty minutes later, as one of the biggest football fans around, Bryce was still going on about the virtues of the Pac 10 conference versus the Big 10. She rolled her eyes as she caught a few phrases regarding the "Ducks," Bryce's beloved alma mater on the western side of the state.

Sarah groaned. "He's lost to me now, isn't he?"

Shaking the memories of the upsetting images, Allison focused on her sister and smiled. "Oh yeah, Bryce meets someone with a Y chromosome who played college football? Good luck getting your husband back anytime soon."

Sarah studied Peter, who politely listened as Bryce quoted running back stats like Rain Man. "So that's the guy from last week? The car accident? The guy I saw at the hospital?"

Allison nodded.

"The one you had a vision of when you touched him?"

"Yeah, that's the guy."

"Seems nice."

Allison crossed her arms over her chest. "They all do, until I see their deaths."

Sarah lifted her arms, paused, and then hugged her around the neck. "Oh, Al, you'll get this all figured out."

"Sure I will."

What a joke. All she wanted was a normal man in her life, only those crazy visions kept intruding. No escape from visions, no intimacy. A pretty good rule, if you considered the alternative. But what about this newfound ability to block others' visions? Could she live a normal life, or was she only setting herself up for even worse pain and failure later?

Enough of this stupid prison.

Enough of letting fear dominate her life.

She squared her shoulders and took in a deep breath of cool, spring air. Sharp and alive, the scent of soil and pine filled her nostrils.

"I'm sick of living like a hermit, terrified of the next painful vision. Now that I can block them, it's time to start living."

"No time like the present, right?"

"Pardon?"

"Uh, I'm certain by 'time to start living' you meant that you'd take Quincy off my hands for a few hours. Bryce and I could use some adult time."

"Adult time, like to discuss the latest bestseller on the list?"

"Something like that." Sarah called to Quincy, who dashed over.

Allison braced herself mentally and patted her niece on the head. "Want me to take you home?"

Quincy twirled on the tiptoes of her cleats. "The long way home?"

"If you mean stopping at the drive-through for ice cream, then yes."

"Yippee!"

Peter and Bryce strolled up, still discussing football. Speaking of trapped, her brother-in-law was not relenting with the verbal onslaught of statistics. When Peter winked, her belly flip-flopped.

Sarah hugged her daughter and pushed her toward Allison with a grin. "Quincy, listen to your Auntie Al. And don't spill anything in her car." Hand in hand, Sarah and Bryce walked away.

Quincy grabbed Allison's hand, chattering about her day. With Peter on the other side of Ivy, they all strolled toward the street. Allison relaxed her guard, and Peter nodded at her polite noises of acknowledgement as Quincy prattled nonstop. Despite the queasy feeling from earlier that afternoon, Allison's cheeks warmed beneath his playful glance. Ivy eagerly tugged on her leash, seeking the next adventure.

Allison felt the tingle begin.

No. God, no.

She frantically tried to put up her mental shield and let go of Quincy, who, for her part, persisted with a strong grip and continued her monologue, oblivious to Allison's distress.

Allison couldn't get enough air. She could no longer see; the power of the developing vision blinded her. As they stepped onto the street, she didn't register the sound of squealing tires.

The next thing she knew, Peter grabbed her and Quincy by the arms, lifted them into the air, and yanked them backward. They sprawled on concrete while he somehow remained upright, balanced on the balls of his feet. She looked up in time to see Ivy fly backward with a sickening thud and a yelp. Ivy lay on her side, leg bent at an awkward angle, whimpering.

The sedan swerved within a few feet of them and sped off.

"Peter, is Quincy all right?"

He nodded curtly, picking up an uninjured Quincy in his arms, a dangerous expression on his face.

Nursing a sore hand, Allison crawled to her dog. Ivy lifted her head and whined. Allison ran her hands over her flank, hearing a yelp when she touched her lower leg and abdomen. Blood dripped from Ivy's mouth.

Standing in a crouch over Allison, Peter's heat radiated in intense waves that washed over her. That furious rage pinged like sleet on her mental connection. The picture of protective anger, Peter cradled a crying Quincy to his shoulder.

People swarmed around, offering help. Sarah and Bryce shouldered their way through the crowd.

"Honey, are you all right?" Sarah cried.

Peter deposited a frightened Quincy into her mother's arms. "Maybe a scrape on the ground, but the car didn't hit her," he said. "Ivy's hurt."

Allison appreciated how his protective stance shielded her from the press of the crowd. Tears rolled down her cheeks as she looked up at him, now a vengeful silhouette against the cloudy sky. He leaned halfway over Allison and Ivy, glaring all the bystanders into keeping their distance. If the echoes in her mind were accurate, he was either about to bolt after the car that nearly hit them or kill anyone who approached them.

"Please help me." Her heart was breaking into pieces as her beloved dog struggled to breathe.

He knelt next to her. She flinched as his eyes turned a cold, lethal black. A muscle in his jaw jumped. "Where's your car?"

"Right across the street."

His voice was calm. Too calm. "Go open the back door."

With a wince, she got to her feet.

He picked up massive Ivy as if she were a tiny puppy, careful of her leg, and laid her on the partially folded-down back seats and the trunk.

Allison climbed in with Ivy and handed Peter the keys. "Please?" She nearly wept, checking back to reassure herself that Quincy was okay.

He wordlessly closed the back door.

...

Peter had to get out of here. Too many people. Too much attention. His desire to kill someone was overwhelming the need to protect Allie.

When he sensed someone jog up and put his hand out, Peter spun and nearly took Bryce's head off. *Damn it, stay calm.*

It took Bryce a minute to get the words out. "Thank you for saving my baby's life." His voice cracked. "I'll find the bastard who did this." He motioned to the back window, where they saw Ivy's eyes, glazed with pain.

Peter nodded as Bryce ran back to his daughter and wife.

White-hot rage threatened to consume him. He couldn't think. *Focus on Allie.*

He started the car. "Where am I going?" He didn't mean to come off sounding like a drill sergeant, but that tone was the best he could manage right now.

At her directions, he carefully navigated the crowded street. Once clear of the sports complex, he drove as quickly as he dared to the vet hospital. His heart turned as he heard Ivy whine, a light thump of her tail, and Allie's murmurs of reassurance.

Pulling up to the front entrance, he raced around to open the rear door, and Allie scrambled out. He gathered Ivy up in his arms once more and strode through the clinic door she held open. The receptionist waved them to the back and called for the veterinarian on duty, Dr. Sampson. Peter eased Ivy down on a metal exam table.

A young man, about thirty, ran into the exam room, taking in the injured dog, Allie, and Peter. "Al, what happened?"

"Someone hit her outside the sports complex a few minutes ago," she said. Her hands shook as she stroked Ivy's head. "I think it's her leg, and maybe more."

Dr. Sampson quickly assessed Ivy and called out orders to the vet tech. "Please set an IV, prep the OR. Let's get a quick x-ray of her leg, chest, and abdomen."

"Do you need me to help?" she asked.

He gave her a professional smile. "That's okay."

The tech deftly threaded the IV line into the dog's front leg. Ivy didn't flinch but lay still on the table, her breathing becoming shallower.

Dr. Sampson looked up. "You're welcome to stay, but I'll work faster if you wouldn't mind waiting in the reception area."

"Absolutely. Please help her." She gave her dog a kiss on the head and backed away, bumping into Peter.

He wrapped his hands over her shoulders to steady her, fighting the urge to fully wrap her in his arms. *Not here. Not yet.*

The receptionist escorted them back to the waiting area and offered coffee. Allie and Peter sat in silence. Eventually, she took in a shaky breath, rolling her neck and shoulders.

"Ivy's in good hands now," he said.

"It's not just that."

"Then what? The man from the park?"

"Not even that."

"What?"

"Back on the street, I got a vision from Quincy." She buried her face in his chest.

No! Her statement slammed into him like a Mack truck. This madness, all of it, had to stop. His hand squeezed her arm so tightly, Allie whimpered. He forced himself to relax his grip and focus on the woman beside him. Peter tucked her more firmly into his chest, welcoming the softness of her body pressed against him. He wanted nothing more than to shelter her forever.

Forever?

There's no forever for me.

Well, actually, there *was* forever, and that was the problem. As only a shade of a man, he had nothing to offer Allie or any woman.

Aware that the receptionist watched them a little too closely, he eased Allie away. At some point, her emotional state would appear out of proportion with what others would assume was grief for an injured pet. "Want to get out of here for a little while?"

With a shaky nod, she collected herself and pasted on a professional guise as they approached the desk. "I'd like to get some fresh air. Would you please give me a call when Ivy's out of surgery, or if her condition changes?" she asked the receptionist.

"Of course. Your number's in the system. Get a little rest and maybe something to eat." When she smiled winningly at Peter, he ignored the woman's interested gaze. He wanted only one woman, and even that desire was wrong.

In the car, the silence wrapped around them like a heavy, wet blanket. Allie pressed her fingers to the bridge of her nose and sighed. He hated seeing this lovely woman's beaten expression.

As he reached out to touch her face, he checked himself and curled his hand into a fist on his lap instead. "Can I drive you somewhere?"

She jumped. "No, I don't, doesn't—" Abruptly turning to him, she said, "You must have somewhere you need to be. You don't need to be dragged through this mess today."

"There's no other place I want to be." Damn it all, if he didn't mean it, too.

When he turned the car on, the sound of the whirring heater fan scored the silence. The clouds had increased, turning everything gray and cold. He sat patiently. He had all the time in the world. Literally.

She leaned her head back on the rest. "Could you just drive for a while?"

Her sadness would have broken his heart in any other lifetime but this one. If all Allie would allow him to do was drive her around, he would do it as long as she wished, if only to stay close by her.

He pulled onto Main Street, arbitrarily turning right into light traffic. A few drops of rain hit the windshield. After about fifteen minutes, he made a left-hand turn, traveled under the interstate, and returned on a county road. Fertile valley fields blurred by as they rode in silence. Spotting a turnout that faced the now cloud-covered Wallowa Mountains, Peter pulled off the road.

"Want to talk about it?"

Groaning, she said, "Which part?"

"Any of it." He reached out and touched her cheek.

She flinched, but then relaxed and leaned into his hand. Their connection flared, but not nearly as powerful now.

He savored the soft skin beneath his fingertips. "Did you feel that?"

She blew out a breath. "Only a little. It's becoming second nature to do whatever it is I do to filter the visions. At least with you. I wish I could have done that earlier today. I guess I wasn't ready."

"Not your fault."

"It is my fault if something bad happens to someone I love." She leaned into his palm.

Peter moved his hand from her cheek into her hair and lightly massaged until she closed her eyes with a sigh. He indulged himself in the feel of her silky hair sliding over his rough hand. Not forever, but good enough for now.

"That guy from the park was scary," she said.

"Could you tell anything about him?"

Guilt squeezed like a fist in his chest. He'd brought Jerahmeel's hit man here. But Allie didn't know that. If she did, she wouldn't want anything to do with Peter.

A line formed between her brows as she turned to him. "I thought you'd know. The vibe I got from him felt similar to when I first contacted you."

"That's strange. Can you tell me what you saw?"

"Well, death, of course. But worse than anything I saw in your images." She rubbed her arms. "Awful images of torture, blood everywhere. Women and children screaming, the suffering went on and on and on. One of the images was of a pregnant woman. He killed her and the unborn child. And he *enjoyed* it. Oh God, the screams."

He needed to destroy this sicko who'd set his sights on Allie.

At her shivering, Peter turned up the heat and pointed all the vents toward her. He didn't know anyone from his cadre of coworkers who performed that kind of torture. Most of his ... colleagues ... simply did their job, hoping each kill was the one that would release them from their contract, and then moved on. Obviously, Jerahmeel had recruited someone new, or someone very different. He'd call Dante or Barnaby later and see if they knew anything.

"Anything particularly helpful about the visions of him?"

She pinned him with her gold-flecked, emerald gaze. "Besides the unrelenting anguish?"

He cringed at her sarcastic tone. "Yes."

"Just odds and ends." She stared out the windshield. "That disgusting man's mind was crammed full of depraved torture and blood and guts. But you know what was strange? When I touched Quincy, it was more specific. I heard a scream for help, and then I saw a mountain lake and a glass shoe."

He stilled his hand on her scalp. "Glass shoe?"

She nodded. "No idea what a glass shoe means, but I saw it. Maybe I'm channeling Cinderella or something strange. My power's been changing over the past week, so I'm not completely sure what to believe right now."

"Changing how?"

"More visions, more pain."

When she wouldn't meet his eyes, he let the matter drop. She was hiding something, but he'd find out later. Meanwhile, he was drawing a blank on anything in his world that a glass shoe represented.

"Anything else?" he asked.

She sighed. "The vision happened too fast to pick up details. Everything's mixed up in my head. I can't tell where one vision started and the other one stopped."

"It's okay, probably didn't mean anything."

"What're the chances of that?" She closed her eyes and flicked her hand at him to silence him before he could answer.

When she groaned and leaned her head back, he rubbed her neck, willing her to relax. After seeing what destruction he was capable of, how could she still trust him? He barely trusted himself. As he kneaded the muscles in her neck, he fought the need to wrap her in his arms. He fought a growing, base need to do much more.

I am a sick bastard.

Forcing his thoughts away from his tightening groin, he appreciated the fine features of Allie's face, her long neck and smooth skin, her soft lips. She smelled like fresh, green grass and coffee. He inhaled deeply.

Home.

Damn it all, she smelled like home.

Something he would never have.

With all the evil he had done, he didn't deserve to be near this woman. But as long as he could be here, he'd not betray Allie's trust. He could at least do this one thing and keep her safe.

When her cell phone rang, she jumped, and he tightened his hand on her neck.

She opened her purse and thumbed to answer the phone.

. . .

She pressed the phone to her ear, heart pounding. "Hello?"

"It's Doug Sampson. Ivy's out of surgery."

"Yes?" She met Peter's intense gaze and welcomed his warm hand on her neck.

"I think she'll pull through. Broken hip, which is fixed. She had a tear in the iliac artery on that side as well."

She took a sharp breath. "Was there a lot of blood loss?"

"Yes, but I have a transfusion dog who donated. And I've given Ivy a bunch of fluids." He paused. "If you'd waited any longer, she might've bled out."

"How long will you keep her?"

"A couple days, depending on how she does. She's pretty sedated right now."

"Thank you for everything, Doug." She sagged into Peter's warm hand.

"Glad to help. I'll be here at ten o'clock tomorrow morning if you'd like to come by. The office is closed, but you have my number. Call when you get here and I'll let you in."

"Sounds good. Thanks again."

Allison set down the phone. She was teary all over again.

Peter cleared his throat. "Ivy will be okay?"

"Looks like it."

"That's great news."

All at once, Allison felt exhausted. The week, the day, her dog, the visions, her feelings about Peter, all caught up to her. She couldn't think straight. Too much had happened.

So much for a new, normal life. So much for the steely determination. Her fresh start had lasted all of a nanosecond before all hell had rained back down upon her head. That carefree attitude and fifty cents would buy her a coffee.

"Can I drive you home? I'd like to help," his low voice cut through her thoughts.

She blinked. "I can't impose—"

Being cared for by a man was alien to Allison, but the thought of sitting home alone with that creepy guy from the soccer fields lurking out there, that shook her to the core. For a moment, she considered going to Sarah and Bryce's house, but her presence could lead a stalker to her family. She couldn't place them in harm's way. Maybe for a short period of time, she could pretend to have a nice man in her life. Only he wasn't exactly a man, was he? Still, having Peter around could be a rare opportunity to experience normal companionship.

Normal? With him? What a joke. If you looked it up in the dictionary, right next to the listing for "abnormal" would be her name and Peter's.

Better to end whatever twisted ... God knows what ... that was between them now.

She repeated herself and pulled away from him. "I won't impose." The air in the car stagnated.

Good. She hit the right balance between politeness and flat-out rejection. No need to be a jerk to this guy. It wasn't his fault her brain had short-circuited.

He slid his hand out from under her hair. "It's no imposition. I'd like to keep an eye on things tonight."

"No, but—" Damn this guy. He wasn't following the we-have-no-future script.

Apparently oblivious to her expanding irritation, he continued. "I'll rest better knowing you're safe." He ran a thumb over her cheek, and damn her mutinous nervous system, but she shuddered.

He put his hand back on the steering wheel. "First, I'd like to go by the hotel to pick up a few things." He put both hands on the wheel and studied the sky through the front windshield. "It's threatening to snow, temperature's dropping."

An inappropriate giggle bubbled up. "If I need someone to cut wood, I know who to ask."

A joke. How appropriate, since her entire life was one big chuckle.

Forget her freak-of-nature power. Forget domestic bliss with a normal man. Who was she fooling? Peter was not exactly human. Not only did she need to avoid relationships with normal men on a regular basis, she now had to add supernatural killers to the list of bewares. How fabulous.

He pulled into the hotel parking lot and left the car running. Leaving her to stew in the morass of her unhappiness, he re-emerged with a small bag and a laptop.

Arriving at Allison's house, he parked her car well away from the house and clicked the garage door open.

"Stay put. Lock the car doors. I'll check the house."

Allison nodded. She pressed the lock, scooted into the driver's seat, and peered out into the early evening. Nothing appeared out of place.

Peter paced in front of the house, stooping every so often to touch the ground. He disappeared around the corner.

She held her breath, straining to hear anything outside the car, searching the shadows.

Her heart thudded in her chest. He'd been gone too long.

He finally re-emerged on the other side of the house, his tall frame illuminated by the headlights. The breath she'd been holding came out with a whoosh. He entered the house through the garage door. After what felt like hours, the house lights came on, and then Peter returned and waved her in. As if this was something he did on a regular basis, checking for a stalker. He must have had some military training if her visions about him were true.

In the kitchen, Allison tried to pull out a few items to make a passable dinner but couldn't focus. A spoon dropped to the floor with a loud clatter. When she stooped down, her hand met Peter's.

Connection zinged along her fingertips.

She froze.

He wrapped his hand around hers and gently pulled her up. She felt only buzzing and no pain now with their contact. So much better.

"Stop." His gaze bore into her.

Her heart flipped. "Okay."

"You're exhausted. Why don't you rest for a while?"

His deep voice was a balm to her frayed nerves. His rough thumb rubbed against her palm, sending delightful swirls into her gut, making it hard to think.

"Do you have a frozen pizza?"

Her brain felt like sludge. "As a matter of fact, I do."

"Then go to sleep." His dark brown eyes were warm. "If it's a matter of heating something in the oven, I can manage."

Holding her hand, he led her across the living room and gave her a light push into the bedroom, closing the door behind her. She eyed her bed like a castaway spying a rescue ship. She changed into flannel pants and a tank top and fell onto the covers, asleep before her head hit the pillow.

Chapter 12

Peter listened at the bedroom door. Silence. When he glanced into the room, he could barely make out Allie's small frame engulfed by the duvet, her long hair spread over the pillow. Hell, the entire bedroom smelled fresh, flowery and outdoorsy, just like her. The desire to slip into the bed and wrap himself around her soft body flared. With what he hoped was better judgment, he eased the door closed and walked back to the living room.

In the past twelve hours, his priorities had changed. No longer could he focus solely on his assignment and the Meaningful Kill. Now he had a bigger mission. He had to keep Allie safe and destroy her stalker.

The pizza had finished heating a few minutes ago, and he indulged in a slice of still-steaming pepperoni and cheese. Normally, he didn't care what he ate or even if he ate, but he had heightened senses after meeting Allie, something else he'd have to ask Barnaby to explain.

Another wave of desire to breathe in her sunlight scent swamped him. He fought the compulsion to go back into the bedroom and slide under the covers.

Get a grip.

He sank into the couch cushion, flipping through channels until he dozed off, relaxed. TV shows murmured in the background of his drifting thoughts.

Until a scream pierced the silence.

He reached the bedroom in two steps, wrenched open the door, and flew into her room. The only light came from the living room. Allie sat bolt upright on the bed, her fear echoing in his own mind. He shook his head to clear her residual emotions.

"Allie?" he said softly, not wanting to alarm her further. "I'm going to turn on the light, okay?"

She had drops of sweat on her forehead and upper lip, and her unfocused eyes stared up at him. Another scream looked about to erupt from her lips. The sound of her harsh breaths rasped across his nerves. Nothing and no one else was in the room, but her panic was real.

Unable to stand there, Peter sat on the edge of the bed and pulled her roughly to him. Allie clutched at his shirt, trembling. He smoothed his hands over her hair, willing her to relax, willing himself to calm down. He wanted to fight her demons.

Hell, he *was* one of her demons.

"Allie, it's okay, it's okay," he crooned low. "I'm right here."

He rocked her gently, his chin on her head. It was different from comforting another woman in his arms, years ago. Allison was more vibrant than any woman he'd held before. He tightened his hold, trying to pour reassurance into her and push away the memories of the past.

"A dream," she said, her voice muffled.

Desire spiked down into his gut as her warm exhalation seeped into his shirt, heating his skin. "What did you see?" He tried to focus. He went hard in reaction to her closeness, and he gritted his teeth to retain control.

When she pushed her tousled hair back over her shoulders, the movement tugged her tank top across her breasts. His mouth went dry. He dragged his gaze back to her haunted face.

She took a deep, shuddering breath. "I saw everything, all at once. Torture, death, images over and over. I saw visions from that man, from Quincy, from you. I couldn't make them stop … cold, ice cold, pain, loneliness."

He had nothing to say to help her. He had nothing to make this nightmare end.

He tilted her sweet face to him. Like a man falling toward earth, he couldn't resist Allie's pull. He leaned down and brushed his lips across hers, the echo of her mind resting lightly on the edge of his own consciousness.

Control cracked and then shattered.

Decades of pent-up emotions boiled to the surface.

He groaned and deepened the kiss. Plunging his hands into her silky hair, he tilted her head back to expose the long lines of her delicate neck. He delved into the warm smoothness of her mouth with his tongue, and she responded with a soft moan that escalated his need. He trailed his hands down her back, then up her arms. Holding on at her ribcage, he traced her firm breasts with his thumbs through the cotton tank-top.

When he flicked a finger over a hard nipple, Allie's hands clenched on his back. The pinch of her nails shot pleasure straight into his balls. *Good.* As her hands drifted downward, to the top of his buttocks, he growled deep in his throat, picked her up roughly, and checked himself. He eased her down onto the center of the bed.

She licked her swollen, parted lips.

His mind exploded.

He ripped her tank top apart, shreds of cotton scattering over the mattress. Unable to hold back, he lowered his head, nipping at her breasts as he pressed her down onto the mattress.

She writhed beneath him, the movement driving his need even higher.

Pulling her arms over her head, he rose up, surveying her smooth skin, pink breasts, and shining lips. He had to possess her completely, had to be inside of her, be a part of her.

"Peter," she whispered.

That one word brought him back to reality. The stalker, her images. He was her protector. She'd just woken up. She was vulnerable. A drop of red bloomed on her lip. He'd done that.

Shoving himself away from her, he retreated toward the door. He would not use her body to slake his own desires.

"It's okay, Allie." To his own ears, he sounded desperate. "I'm sorry. You trusted me, and I took advantage. Please forgive me." He backed away until he bumped against the wall, unable to stop staring at her perfect body.

Naked from the waist up, Allie sat up on the bed, pushed her tangled hair back, and stared at him, her emerald and gold eyes pinning him in place. Peter couldn't move.

• • •

Allison didn't know what to do. She craved Peter's touch, his warmth, his protection. In her world of death and evil, this inhuman man had given her strength and security. Beneath his hands, she had blossomed. For tonight, it didn't matter that he had secrets. What mattered were his actions that she had witnessed in the here and now.

Before her dreams had turned ugly this evening, she had imagined him in this bedroom, exactly like this, looking at her with the same desire she saw now.

Peter appeared poised to bolt, but she didn't want him to leave. She felt more human and more complete in his arms than she had with anyone else. Maybe she couldn't control the things happening to her head, but she could make one decision for herself tonight. Before she lost her courage, Allison slid off the bed, scattering the shredded pieces of the tank top. She glanced down at her naked torso, and then slowly raked her gaze up his compact form, lingering a moment on the bulge in his jeans before enjoying the view of his wide chest. When she met his eyes, she stared at him for several seconds, blinked, and licked her lips. She couldn't make her invitation any clearer.

Peter's gaze darkened to pure onyx as she slowly took one step then another toward him. His hands balled into fists. Sweat beaded his forehead. Her semi-naked state should have made her feel shy, but it didn't.

He stood silent and frozen with a stricken expression, eyes narrowed to black slits, head shoved back against the wall. Still he didn't move, didn't touch her, even as she took a slow step and continued to advance toward him.

Stopping inches away from him, Allison brushed her fingertips over his hard jawline, giving him every opportunity to run. He didn't move, but clenched his mouth and shuddered.

She had all of his attention, and she liked it. As she reached under his shirt, he grabbed her wrist, but he didn't hurt her.

"Don't," he ground out, plain desperation written on his features.

Rejection hit her like a slap across the face. "Don't you want me?"

"You have no idea." His voice was raw and angry.

"I'm sorry, I thought—" Suddenly too aware of her nakedness, she tried to pull her arm from his grip, to cover herself. Her cheeks heated.

What a fool I am.

He tightened his grip to just short of pain. "No."

"It's okay. Let go of me. I'll leave you alone." Damn it, if she didn't blink back pricks of tears. She would *not* cry in front of him.

"I don't want you to leave me alone." His voice had turned to gravel, raw suffering infused into each word.

"I don't under—"

His grip on her wrist, like an iron manacle, stretched her arm up and out. "I want you. That's the damn problem."

"So you do want me?"

"Hell, yeah. But I'm no good for you."

Her heart skipped a beat. "Did you ask what I want?"

His jaw dropped.

"Ask me."

Sandpaper wasn't as rough as his growl. "What. Do. You. Want?"

"I want ... " With her free hand, she reached under his shirt and trailed her fingernails over his corded abdomen.

His muscles jumped in response, and she liked it. He held her outstretched arm like a lifeline.

When she touched him, the mental connection clicked into place more comfortably this time, augmenting their physical contact. That mental wind continued to swirl, but now it felt like the texture of his mind. She controlled the depth of the visions more easily and struggled less to maintain a barrier against the mental roar. When she sensed him in her mind, the primary emotion was raw, ravenous hunger. For her.

"Damn, Allie. I'll hurt you. I can't control myself around you."

Tugging at her manacled wrist until he let go, she stood on tiptoes and locked her hands onto his face. "I don't want your control. I want *you*."

"You have no idea what you're asking. If I lose control, I can't hold back my mind. I can't hold back anything." His Adam's apple bobbed with the convulsive swallow. Sweat beaded his forehead. He was as tense as a coiled spring, standing stiff as a statue.

"So don't hold back."

"No. You don't get it. I could destroy you, in here." He pointed to his head. The misery in his hoarse voice cut straight into her soul.

Heart pounding, Allison kissed his lower lip, then guided his hand to her breast. "I trust you."

Something broke behind those black, lost eyes, and he crushed her lips in a bruising kiss. When she pushed his shirt up, he ripped it off. As she traced kisses down his heated chest with her lips, he growled and spun them around, switching positions and pressing her hard into the wall. She sensed the moment when he relaxed his superhuman strength, although his tight embrace still supported her. Could he maintain control of his power without hurting her?

With his muscled thigh pinning her hips in place and his hands fisted in her hair, she was trapped in the most delicious of prisons while he devoured her mouth with kisses. When he opened her mouth wider to explore with his tongue, she gripped the flexed cords on his shoulders. Her head swam as his strong mouth slanted over hers, consuming her body and mind.

Peter stepped back long enough to shove her flannel pajamas down over her hips and away. He leaned into her, keeping her shoulders pressed to the wall while he snaked an arm around the small of her back. Arching her toward him, he ground his hard groin into her hips, the denim jeans abrading her sensitive flesh, sending a bolt of desire right into her gut.

When he pulled his hands out of her hair, she moaned in disappointment, until he trailed a hand down her belly and lower to her soft curls. He stroked lower until she writhed in anticipation. With his knee, he nudged her legs apart and slid his hand lower into her folds. At his first stroke, her legs went weak, and she clutched at his shoulders for support.

His voice slid over her. "I need you."

Allison felt his growing desire beneath the jeans pressed into her abdomen and shivered. "You have me."

As he dove back into her mouth for another soul-shattering kiss, she stroked him through the denim. She unbuckled his jeans and eased them downward; her hands glided over his buttocks and muscled legs. She encountered a knife in a holster strapped to his lower leg, and she stopped, surprised as the knife emitted a faint green glow.

He grabbed her hand, pulling her away. "Hell. Never touch that." Leaning down, he kicked his jeans off, but left the sheathed weapon attached to his leg.

"Why?"

"Just don't. You should never touch the knife."

Her next question was smothered beneath his warm lips. He literally took her breath away.

When she pressed into his hard erection, he groaned. Yanking her hands up and onto his shoulders, he reached under her hips and lifted her, scraping her back against the wall. Allison wrapped her legs around his waist and held on behind his neck, kissing him over and over.

He lowered her, their sweat-slicked skin connecting them, chest to chest. When she felt his wet tip at her entrance, she whimpered. An electricity of a different kind thrummed through her body. He guided her hips into position and pushed her down onto him, driving in deeply.

She gasped, suddenly stretching to accept him. His heat warmed her to the core.

He pumped into her slowly at first then faster, pinning her between the hard, cold wall and the unyielding furnace of his body. His strong hands guided her hips with the mounting rhythm. The windstorm of their connected minds and how easily he supported her body weight despite his thrusts sparked pleasure deep inside her—this had to be like flying.

As she crested, he leaned against her, kissing her hard, his tongue filling her mouth, each thrust of his hips more forceful than the last. She cried out, clawing at his neck in ecstasy, and he followed moments later.

Arms weak, she shuddered with aftershocks as he shifted. His leonine smile turned her heart over, and something poignant and sharp caught when she took a deep breath.

She shivered when he trailed a hand down her side and under her bottom and thigh.

A tiny sigh escaped her lips as he eased her hips away, lowering her feet to the floor but keeping her flush to his hard, hot body.

The air was cool on her damp back when Peter scooped her up and deposited her in bed, crawling in after her.

Tucking in against her backside, he pulled her deep into his embrace and wrapped corded arms around her.

She'd never felt so safe, so cherished, and so complete. Over her shoulder, she kissed him deeply. For a split second, she caught a glimpse of a normal, passionate relationship.

Only nothing about this situation was normal—not her freakish powers, not the superhumanly strong killer laying next to her in the bed. With a yawn, she drifted off into a dreamless, exhausted, but uneasy sleep.

Chapter 13

Peter drifted, semi-awake, aware of the amazing woman in his arms. He didn't move for fear of disturbing her and simply watched her sleep. He wanted to breathe in her sweetness like this for as long as possible. Was this how Barnaby had felt about his wife, that he would do anything for her? Like ... break the contract?

Damn it, he wasn't going to entertain that kind of magical thinking. He preferred to think about how perfectly Allie fit him.

Even now, with her sound asleep, he sensed the low-level electricity of their mental connection, though it didn't overwhelm either of them anymore. Now it felt familiar, like wearing a favorite piece of clothing or having a friend nearby.

Yet there was also the reality of Allie doubled over on the concrete, her face tear-streaked, earlier today. What kind of future did she have with him? His presence put her at risk from Jerahmeel or his associates. Beyond the amazing sex, Peter had nothing else to offer, other than unending suffering. How could he lead her on, when he had no realistic hope of a long-term relationship?

Hell.

When he tightened his grip, she murmured in her sleep and stirred.

The only light came from the living room, and her face was cast in shadow when she rolled back and touched his stubbled face with one finger. A bolt of desire shot into his groin. Reveling in the sensation of her smooth body next to his, he leaned on one arm and kept his other arm around her small frame.

"Peter, I ... "

"Shh." He brushed her swollen lips with his thumb and then dropped a light kiss onto them.

"I feel ... " Allie's grumbling stomach interrupted her.

He laughed. "Hungry?"

When she leaned over and turned on the bedside lamp, he froze. On her back were abrasions where her soft skin had torn. At his expletive, she turned around, perplexed.

"Hell." He gently pressed her onto her stomach and examined her back. Red scratches bloomed against her fair skin. He ran a finger over one and she flinched. "Allie, your back. I had no idea."

She peered up at him over her shoulder. "It's okay."

"No, it's not. I told you I couldn't control … "

She rolled back toward him, her breasts pressed enticingly together. He dragged his gaze to her face, expecting to see accusation there. If he couldn't keep from hurting this woman, then he deserved the blame.

Instead, she smiled. "If you want to blame someone, I'll give you the name of the general contractor who built this house."

"What?"

"Knockdown wall treatment. Much rougher on skin than regular flat walls. Who would've thought?"

She maintained a deadpan expression until she broke into peals of laughter. Peter shocked himself by suddenly laughing as well, a sound foreign to him.

"Let me grab a quick shower, and then maybe we can have some pizza."

Still dissatisfied that he had put a mark on her, he agreed. "I'll heat it up."

He couldn't take his eyes off her lithe frame as she rolled out of bed and, naked, flitted to the bathroom, flipped on the light, and closed the door. The shower started.

Jealous of the water sluicing over her body, he hardened. With a groan, he rolled out of bed and pulled on his clothes, using brute willpower not to join her in the shower.

Fifteen minutes later, the microwave beeped as she entered the kitchen, her hair towel-dried and tendrils curling. He inhaled the scent of flowers from her shampoo.

"Smells great." She pushed up her sweatshirt sleeves; she was endearing in wool socks and sweatpants.

"I agree." He picked up a damp strand of her hair and put it to his nose. Her pinkening cheeks were a treat.

After they enjoyed the reheated pizza, she sat back, satisfied, and rubbed her flat belly. "Perfect dinner."

"This is the best I've felt in as long as I can remember." It was certainly the most human he'd felt in forever.

She was silent for a moment. "So what *are* you?" Nodding toward the bedroom, she added, "The images I see of you? The knife? I'm justified in asking." She glanced at his leg.

He dragged his hands over his face. Where to start?

"So the short answer is I made a very bad deal many years ago and am still paying for that decision today. I was born in 1915 near Columbus, Ohio." Now he had her attention. He cringed at her speculative raised eyebrow. "Yes, that means I'm very old."

Pushing the chair back, he rested a hand on his crossed leg. "So I was a teenager during the Great Depression, but my parents always wanted me to go to college. I attended Ohio State and got an ROTC scholarship in the 1930s. Right when I was accepted into the master's program in history in 1941, Japan bombed Pearl Harbor."

Allie leaned an elbow on the table and propped her chin on her fist.

Peter let himself relax a small amount. At least she wasn't running for the door. Yet.

"The army let me finish my degree in May of 1943. I walked across the stage, received my diploma, and headed off to Fort Bragg the same day."

"Wow, that's quick."

"Many men had similar experiences. After infantry officer training, I shipped out to France a year later, served behind the lines for a few months, then got sent to the front for the Battle of the Bulge."

Her green eyes widened. "Either you're completely delusional or this is one disturbing story."

"I wish I were delusional."

And he hadn't even tackled the part he dreaded. But she needed to know.

"So I was commanding a platoon in the Ardennes, December 1944, in miserable conditions. We got dumped right in the thick of the fighting. The death tolls were horrendous, on both sides. In one attack, we managed to ambush a German platoon and kill most of them in hand-to-hand combat."

He rubbed absently at his right arm. "As I searched for survivors, a German officer shot me in the arm, so I killed him." He indicated his watch with the worn leather band and scratched face. "I kept this as a souvenir although I never expected to have the watch for quite this long. They transferred me to Ravenel Field Hospital in France when infection set in. Thankfully, penicillin had come into use during the war or I might've lost my arm. I ended up having surgery a few days later to get rid of dead tissue and was discharged due to nerve damage in my arm."

She pressed her lips together. "Your arm seems to work well now."

"I'm getting to that part. So what I haven't mentioned yet is the woman I left behind in Ohio. Claire."

"Is that the woman in my visions?"

He nodded, his memories bittersweet. "Sweet girl—we dated in college, and she waited for me until I returned from France. After I was discharged from the army, we got married, in the summer of 1945. We were eager to start a family, but right after the wedding, she contracted polio while visiting relatives in Illinois."

Tapping her chin, Allie said, "Adult-onset polio was supposed to be much worse."

Yes, it was. He could still hear the drone of the iron lung bellows compressing air in and out to aid Claire's pitiful, exhausted efforts to breathe. The only part of her visible, her sweat-covered head, was bound at the neck by rubber gaskets.

Lying flat on her back, trapped in the depths of the machine, she could only communicate in broken sentences timed with the rhythm of the bellows, and even that became too difficult. Her world boiled down to a sterile hospital room and a mirror angled over her head to see the visitors and attendants when they spoke with her. That iron lung sealed her in as surely as a metal coffin.

"She was suffering, and the doctors told me she wouldn't survive. I needed to settle her personal matters."

"How awful." Allie covered her mouth with her hand.

"Well, I wasn't about to prepare her last will and plan for her imminent death. I got mad, really mad. Like drunk and screaming-in-the-streets, pissing mad. Here I'd survived the war—hell, survived the Ardennes—and now the woman I loved would be dead soon? No, sir. I refused to accept it."

When Allie reached over and squeezed his hand, he focused on the gold flecks in her green eyes. Despite being long-lived and superhumanly strong, he'd never told anyone the entire story of Claire, never shared the pain his decision caused every time he remembered his wife's suffering, tear-streaked face. Something about Allie sitting here and listening with seeming acceptance shored up his strength.

"Apparently running around the streets yelling that I would do anything to save my wife attracted attention. The wrong kind of attention."

"I don't understand."

Releasing her hand, he rubbed his face. "I ended up in an alley with a dapper-looking man named Jerahmeel. He looked like a slick salesman, fancy gold rings and chains, oiled hair. But he promised me he could save my wife. What did I have to lose? I was drunk. So I signed some paper Jerahmeel put in front of me without reading it, shook his hand, told him to go right ahead and try to save my wife, even wished him every success with his efforts."

"And?"

"Damned if she didn't get out of that iron lung within the week. Walked shortly after that. Doctors said it was a miracle."

He stared past the wood grain on the kitchen table—if only he'd appreciated that brief halcyon time before his real life ended and hell truly began.

Allie cleared her throat. "But?"

"A few months later, Jerahmeel knocked on my front door and told me it was time to pay up. That was the last time I saw my wife."

"What?"

"I told Claire I was going out for a drink with an old friend. I still remember the look on her face. She knew something wasn't right and tried to make me tell her what was going on. I wasn't allowed to say anything. So I lied. The last time I saw her, she was yelling and crying. And I never went back. God knows what she thought of me.

"Then I was in a cold cave somewhere. Jerahmeel strapped the knife to my leg and explained that I had, indeed, made a formal deal with the devil. I always thought that was a figure of speech. I was dead wrong."

"There really are deals with the devil?"

Pointing a thumb at his chest, he frowned. "I'm living proof."

"Jerahmeel is the devil?" Her green gaze bore into him.

"Pretty much. He's the human representation of Satan in this world. And he has the power to destroy. He has the power to command those who are under his control—under contract. He requires me to find and kill bad people and trap their souls' energy into this knife. Jerahmeel feeds off the energy. It's how he survives. And there's something extra-special about criminal souls that are tastier. The more evil, the better, as far as he's concerned. The knife gets hungry when he's hungry." He motioned toward his lower leg.

The condemnation in her eyes hurt like a spear in his chest. "So what I saw? That was you, killing people? On command?"

He was so tired.

She didn't understand his struggle. Why should she? It didn't make sense to him, even after all these years.

"I have no choice, Allie. I'm what is called an Indebted. Jerahmeel owns me. I have to kill. The only way to break the contract is to make what is called a Meaningful Kill. Dammit, I've tried that numerous times. I enlisted for the Korean Conflict, Vietnam, and the Gulf and Iraq wars, trying to kill as many bad guys as possible, hoping that each time would be my last murder. I've tracked down rapists, serial killers, and pedophiles. You name the heinous crime, I've exterminated the perpetrators. Nothing. No Meaningful Kill. Still under contract."

She shoved her chair back. "I don't believe this. You can't be a cold-blooded killer." Her eyes glistened.

"If it's any consolation, the only people I kill are people who are bad." It even sounded lame. Like how he'd justified his actions for decades now. Damn Jerahmeel and damn this cursed job.

"Why only criminals?"

"Jerahmeel is compelled by certain rules. I don't know all of them myself. But my friend Barnaby has known him for centuries. Jerahmeel might be powerful, but he is limited in how he can replenish that power."

Crossing her arms, she said, "Sounds like a convenient excuse to commit murder."

"I agree it sounds that way. But there's nothing I can do about it."

Silence descended on the kitchen. He couldn't even hear her breathing, though her chest rose and fell beneath the sweatshirt.

There it was: bleak, blank nothingness. He saw nothing when he considered a future with Allie. She was correct. He had no good answers for her, nothing to commend him as a man. Nothing to offer anyone.

A tear rolled down her cheek and landed on her arm. "Do you have an assignment to kill me?"

"No!" he roared, jumping to his feet. "I would never hurt you, I swear."

Dammit, she flinched away from him.

"What if you were compelled by this Jerahmeel guy?" Her voice shook.

"I wouldn't do it. Besides, you're not a bad person. You're not a criminal."

"But I thought you had to kill whoever he chooses?"

All good questions. "Sometimes it's his choice, and sometimes it's mine. But I would rather die first than hurt you."

"Aren't you dead now?" The question hung heavy in the air between them.

"Not exactly. I was human until the day Jerahmeel got hold of me, but I'm not dead. I'm something in between. It's virtually impossible for me to die. I guess it's possible, but difficult. As you know, my healing rate is fast. We apparently don't age, either."

"Are there others out there like you?"

"Yes."

"How many?"

"I don't know. But most of them have been around a lot longer than I have."

Her fingers shook as she tucked a strand of hair behind her ear. "So you may walk the Earth for, what, hundreds of more years?"

"There's a good chance I'll still be here many years from now."

Peter couldn't meet her eyes.

• • •

Leaving him to stand next to the table, Allison jumped up and walked to the cabinet, took out a bottle of red wine, and attempted to open it. Damn it, her hands trembled. She couldn't hang on to the bottle. Tears spilled down her cheeks.

"Here."

She startled.

Peter had moved behind her. With steady hands, he uncorked the bottle and poured them both a glass.

She downed hers in two gulps, nodding at him to pour another. She didn't care about his somber expression as he filled her glass. She took another swig.

Swiping at her damp cheeks, she cursed her stupid emotions. Allowing herself to feel this deeply was what got her into this morass in the first place. "So who're you here to kill in this dangerous town of La Grande?"

Her tone was sarcastic, and she didn't care. All she wanted was a nice man in her life, some affection, safety, and companionship. Someone who wouldn't die after she saw visions of him. Apparently, that was too much to ask.

Actually, in a twisted way, she'd gotten her just desserts. Allison had landed herself a grade-A, half-dead, devil-possessed murderer—apt punishment for predicting her father's death years ago, and all the subsequent deaths. The tears started fresh again, and they ran unchecked.

She lifted her glass for another splash of wine. "You didn't answer my question. Who are you here to kill?"

"I think it's the man who's stalking you."

"You don't know for sure?" Her voice rose a notch and cracked. "Shouldn't you, like, confirm who's supposed to die before you start killing folks?"

"It's not that easy this time. Jerahmeel's toying with me. I'm not sure why. But yes, I believe my next kill is the man you saw earlier today."

Hysterical laughter bubbled up. "Fantastic. So we could be part of a demented riddle? Maybe you're not here to kill the guy who wants to kill me. Maybe you are. So this guy is like you, right?"

"He's nothing like me!" Peter growled, leaning toward her.

She should've been nervous. His eyes turned jet-black and heat radiated from him. Tense lines formed at the corners of his mouth as he stared at her. It would be stupid to provoke him. He could tear her apart with his bare hands. But what did it matter?

She pressed forward, choking on inappropriate giggles. "Maybe this stalker guy is the same as you. The images in his mind do feel somewhat similar, though his are a hundred times worse."

Ignoring the vein bulging out on his tense neck, she took another gulp of wine. The surface of the liquid quivered in the glass. "So, if it's 'very difficult' for you to die, then I would presume that this guy is similarly … difficult to kill?"

His lips thinned to a white line before he replied. "I think we have to assume that yes, he is difficult to kill. This guy seems to be similar to me but perhaps stronger, as best I can tell." He spoke too quietly, too calmly.

"So he appears to be stronger than anything you've seen before?" She hiccupped and poked a finger hard into Peter's rock-hard chest.

A muscle in his jaw jumped.

She had passed the point of caring if she hurt him two glasses of wine ago. "What makes you think you can kill him"—poke, poke—"before he kills me … or runs over any other family members?"

Peter's stunned silence dragged at the air between them.

He blinked, his eyes remaining black. "That's a decent question. I don't know. But I promise I will protect you."

"I don't think that you can." She finished the glass, off-balance. Defeated. Her head started to swim. "Really, it doesn't matter if he kills me. All I've done with my life is predict other people's deaths. What a useless skill."

He opened his mouth, then closed it with a click of teeth.

She laughed mirthlessly. "Now, thanks to my *gift*, I have a clear idea of how this guy will torture me. All I have to do is wait around for it to happen. Now there's something to look forward to."

"Allie, please."

"What do I have to live for anyway? To predict more deaths? No, thank you."

He stretched out his hand and then dropped it.

His lost expression was even funnier considering he'd faced down bayonets, German tanks, North Koreans, Punji sticks, Scud missiles, and IEDs. But he had no clue how to handle a hysterical woman. Hilarious.

She raised her hand. "Oh, wait, I'm not done yet." The last swig of wine in her glass tasted sour. "My dog's been run over, and I welcomed a not-quite-human into my bed. And I'm having death visions of my six-year-old niece. Which, by the way, my visions *always* come true. Always. Did I cover everything?" She reached for the wine bottle again. "Life just doesn't get any better than this cluster."

She held up her hand as he opened his mouth to speak. "No. I tried to make a fresh start. I tried to have normal. It makes no difference what I do, this shit keeps coming right back."

"Allie ... " He intercepted her arm.

As she struggled against his iron grip, he tried to pull her into his arms, but the dam burst at his steady touch.

Sobbing, Allison pounded on his shoulders. All the years of pain poured out of her. Anger and helpless terror drove her as she hit him on the chest, her weak slaps loud in the quiet house. She had never hit another person in her entire life.

He stood there, arms loosely encircled around her, absorbing her blows without flinching. His forehead crinkled with worry, or was it pity? Those black eyes, while directed at her, had become lifeless, shuttered.

After she spent her energy, she cried, exhausted and limp, as he held her. How long he stood there, patiently letting her sob into his shirt, her foggy brain had no idea.

She straightened up. Clarity steamrolled her into sobriety.

There would be no more crying on his shoulder.

Stepping out of his arms, she forced herself to look at his handsome, sad face; the tenderness there hurt even more. But she'd made her decision. Time to rip off the Band-Aid.

"You need to leave."

His eyes widened. "I don't understand."

"I can't do this." She touched her chest and waved her hand at him. "Us. Together. In here, my head. Any of it."

"What?"

"Look, I'm sorry for what you went through. I'm sorry if I led you on. But there is no future for us. For me."

His Adam's apple bobbed twice, then his eyes hardened into obsidian beneath the angry slash of his dark eyebrows.

"I see." He spun on his heel and stormed out faster than she could follow with her eyes.

After the front door slammed shut, the entire house shuddered into silence.

• • •

"Have you finished your assignment, Anton?" The way he asked made it clear he already knew the answer.

"No, my lord Jerahmeel. But—"

"But nothing! Get the job done." Jerahmeel adjusted his curled and oiled black locks in his vehicle's rearview mirror. "I'm getting hungry, and I hate losing an employee." One pinky finger smoothed his eyebrows. "The loss of Barnaby is too fresh. And Blackstone's too close to his Meaningful Kill. If things continue, he's going to figure it out."

Anton couldn't keep the instructions straight. "At first you only wanted me to check on Blackstone to make sure he hadn't blown his cover by that lame car crash. Then that yummy lady came along who might make him want to quit his job. Now you want me to kill him?"

"No, you *imbécile!*" Jerahmeel snapped, his deep voice inhumanly augmented. The windows shook. "Blackstone is already contemplating how to end his contract. The woman gives him even more reason. You need to take away that reason for wanting his contract to end.

"There's something about her that feels familiar and tasty. The mere scent of her whetted an appetite I didn't know I had. She's his inspiration to end the contract, and you know how I feel about contracts ending. It's so rude."

"She was nice. When I touched her, all the bad things went away," Anton said.

"What?"

"It felt awesome. Like I was flying and full from a nice meal and free from any future assignments." He tap, tap, tapped on his forehead, the rhythm soothing him. "Felt great."

"Peter withheld that piece of information from me. Bad Peter. Maybe that's why I was attracted to her scent. Fascinating. And she's with Blackstone." Jerahmeel smoothed his neatly pressed silk slacks. "Even more reason to get rid of her."

"What is she?"

"She's a Ward. They can identify us."

"That's not good."

"No, of course not. Even more reason to get rid of her." A black expression crossed his unlined face. "Well, then, you'd best get to it and eliminate Blackstone's reason for living. I need to keep all my little pawns in the game. I hate to lose a piece."

Anton picked at his fingernails, cuticles bleeding. "But can I ... can I still have fun?"

"Yes, yes, of course. But quit wasting my time. Finish your task so we can return to business as usual. I need all of my employees back out there so I can feed.

"Make it hurt, though. Especially Blackstone. Hurt him badly. But don't kill him. Understand?"

Chapter 14

Allie's words stung more than her weak blows to Peter's body.

Her assessment was totally correct: he *was* a cold-blooded murderer. The fact that he killed for the good of society only masked the hypocrisy. Trapped within a contract, he killed humans. End of story. All the rationalizing in the world wouldn't change that reality.

The expression on her swollen, tear-streaked face had hit him like a torpedo.

Then she had told him to leave.

Damn it, walking out of that house was the hardest thing he'd done since leaving Claire. It brought back the anguish he'd buried since the day he'd shoved a hat on his head and crossed over the worn rug in the entrance to the small house he shared with Claire.

Now Allie had rolled up her welcome mat.

As he stood outside on her porch, his hands clenching and unclenching next to the handle of the front door, he broke out in a cold sweat.

All he could do was keep her safe. He could offer nothing more. This woman deserved a lifetime with a partner who loved her. She deserved someone whole, not the shadow of a man he'd become, not the killer hiding behind a mission.

Once he had ensured her safety, he would leave forever.

Seriously, what had he been thinking? For a moment, he'd imagined his future, and it had Allie in it. But she had destroyed that fantasy, made it abundantly clear what she thought of him. Fair enough, he couldn't argue that she was inaccurate.

But damn how her words shredded him like someone had flayed his skin raw.

For now, he needed to follow through on his promise to keep her safe, no matter if she wanted him to or not. His leaving her house wouldn't protect her. Quite the opposite. So he was in for a chilly night, even for someone like him who wasn't affected by the weather.

He began to pace a wide circle through the woods and across the gravel lane to her house. The night was not late enough. There were far too many hours until morning to be alone with his thoughts.

• • •

Allison's head throbbed. Her eyelids must have been coated with sandpaper. The clock read seven in the morning, but it felt as though she hadn't slept at all.

Flopping over on the bed, she put a pillow over her head and groaned. Passion up against the bedroom wall. Peter's bizarre story. The revelation that she'd almost trusted a cold-blooded killer. Almost believed there was a chance for a relationship with this man. Only he wasn't a normal man, was he? No more than she was a normal woman, truth be told.

She had surmised something along those lines from the visions she'd gotten off him, but having him tell the story so matter-of-factly made the truth all too real. At some point she must have made it back to the bed and passed out, since she was still in the clothes from the previous evening.

After washing up, she dressed in jeans and a sweater. An inch or so of snow was on the ground already, and she didn't welcome the idea of going out in the cold, even if it was to see Ivy.

Twenty minutes later, Dr. Sampson motioned her into the boarding area. "Come on back, Al. Ivy's resting over here."

With a tired yip, Ivy tried to get up from where she lay in her enclosure in the dog ward. Her tail thumped against the metal walls. She whined.

"Ivy!" Allison ran over to open the door and crouched down to hug her dog's massive head. Tears pricked Allison's eyes.

Ivy licked her hands and face and gave her a sideways doggy grin, her tail thwacking the enclosure walls. Bandages covered Ivy's abdomen, and her hip and leg were casted.

"She'll be fine," Dr. Samson said. "I'd like to observe her for a few more days to make sure her gut is working well and force her to rest that hip. But she should be back to mischief soon. I think the hardest part will be ensuring that she doesn't overdo it."

Allison nodded. Ivy's energy was boundless, and her dog would hurt herself in an effort to play. "Mind if I sit with her for a while?"

"Not at all, I'm just doing rounds. Let me know when you leave."

"Thanks again for saving her."

"My pleasure." He closed the door behind him.

Allison gave Ivy a good scratch behind her ears and received more affectionate licks. It did her soul good to see her faithful companion recovering from her injuries.

The tingling in the back of Allison's head began at a low-level rumble, and she frowned, trying to focus harder and identify its source. She couldn't quite get at it. Like a memory beyond recollection, or something she'd forgotten.

A wall of terror and pain slammed into her like a locomotive. Flashes of pictures flew through her mind. She couldn't stop it. Too much. Too fast. Ice-cold suffering. The images kept coming, overwhelming her sight, her hearing, her brain. She struggled to get up off the floor.

"I don't—" She cringed, knees buckling.

"Help."

• • •

Peter's cell phone rang as he climbed into the truck. After Allie had left her house, he'd run to town to pick up his truck. Of course, he'd lost her on the way. His kind was fast in short bursts, but not as fast as a car when it came to piling up miles. Like all Indebted, he had limits to his hell-blessed abilities.

"It's Dante, bro, where are you?"

"I'm in La Grande. What's going on?"

"Something weird. I called in for another assignment and was told no assignments for now. Jerahmeel said he's working on a special project. When I asked what it was, Big Boss just laughed and said it involved you."

Peter gripped the cell phone. "I don't understand."

"Me neither, so I called Barnaby."

"Why?"

"He knows everything."

Peter couldn't argue that point.

"Barnaby said you must be close to being free, because that's what happened to him. They threw the whole kit and caboodle at him."

"What does 'kit and caboodle' entail?"

Dante paused. "Dude, you're going up against a minion. Jerahmeel's hand-selected enforcer."

"Never heard of a minion."

"According to Barnaby, they only show up to make it miserable or impossible for you to finish your contract. The one Barnaby had to destroy was especially nasty."

Peter shoved his free hand through his hair. "But it's possible."

"Sure, but they're bent on the destruction of anything you hold dear in the meantime. They'll take away any motivation you might have to fight back. Any motivation to get out of your contract."

Allie.

Peter's hand balled into a fist. "What am I supposed to do?"

"Keep that pretty doctor safe and be ready." Dante paused again. "Actually, bro, I was going to visit. I'm bored. And who knows? I might be able give you a hand."

"Isn't that against the rules?"

"No idea. Don't care. What's he going to do, make my life a living hell?" His laugh had no mirth. "But seriously, I don't want to see you dead-dead. And I don't like that this minion may try and take out innocents. I may be a bastard, but I will not sit by while women get hurt."

"I agree."

"Where's your lady friend now?"

"She was supposed to stop by the vet hospital this morning. I don't know where she is now."

"She's alone?" The fear in his voice alarmed Peter. Nothing scared Dante.

"Uh, yes."

"Go find her! Don't let her out of your sight until we get there."

"Who's we?"

Dante had already clicked off the line.

• • •

Peter tried not to attract undue attention as he supported most of Allie's body weight, guiding her out of the clinic and into her car. She doubled over several times, and would have fallen if it weren't for his holding her upright.

Her torment had acted like a beacon in his own mind, drawing him right to the clinic.

"Talk to me." Her shaking hands were ice-cold. He blasted the heater, turning all vents toward her.

"Too much." Panting, she rubbed her chest and clutched at the front of her sweater. "Something's wrong. I can't focus. Oh God, it hurts."

"Can you pinpoint anything?" He squeezed her hands, trying to get her attention, trying to do something—anything—to reduce her pain.

The tension left her shoulders and she leaned back in the seat.

"For whatever reason, it's clearer when we're touching." Her breathing slowed down.

"Can't you feel me in your mind?"

"Yes, but you've moved to the background. Right now, there's another big storm of noise in my head. Contact with you calms it down."

"Before, you said touching me had the opposite effect."

"You're right. Here's what I know, though. Since meeting you, my powers have been changing. Is this sensation another cycle of that change?"

He hated to think that somehow he'd been the catalyst for the pain ripping through Allie.

"Possibly." He chafed her hands, maintaining contact. "What do you see?"

She stared with unfocused eyes out the front windshield. "Only a few images. Discomfort, fear, cold. Maybe snow and … a mountain lake. The lake is somehow familiar. I see … the glass slipper again. I don't understand."

The shrill ring of her cell phone brought her gaze into sharp focus. With unsteady hands, Allie thumbed on the phone. "Hi, Sarah." The light tone belied the pain on her face.

After a pause, her lips pressed into a grim line. "Gone? What happened? You checked at her friend's house?" Her knuckles whitened on the phone. "Oh God. Is Bryce out searching?"

Another pause.

"Sarah, about Quincy. I saw something yesterday and again a few minutes ago. A lake. I don't know what it means, or if it's even worth anything. I know, I'm trying to focus, but I'm not getting anything else. If I figure out more, I'll call you. Okay, I love you, too."

She hung up the phone, her features suffused with agony.

"Quincy's missing. She was playing at a friend's house and was supposed to run home, two houses down. She never got there."

Anger and worry congealed in his gut. Who would want to harm that sweet girl?

Hell.

Allie met his stare, her eyebrows raised. She scrabbled for her phone.

"Oh God. I can't be right." She clicked on her sister's number, leaning forward to press her fingers onto the bridge of her nose. "Sarah? One more question. What exactly was Quincy doing at her friend's house?"

Peter heard the reply, right before the phone dropped from her nerveless fingers.

"Playing Cinderella."

Chapter 15

Hollow despair gnawed at Allison while Peter drove back to her house. The Subaru's wheels sprayed wet slush, and sleet pinged off the windshield, punctuated by the squeak of the wipers.

She had to slow down her racing thoughts and focus, but images of the past week competed for attention. She couldn't hold on to one image long enough to examine it.

Frustrated, she leaned forward and groaned.

"What?" He pulled into the garage and turned off the car.

"I'm trying to think through for more details when I touched Quincy, but I can't focus." She struggled to form sentences. "It's like holding on to sand."

He touched her neck, rubbing lightly. "Don't try so hard."

"No, there's too much interference, too many images. It hurts inside my mind."

He came around to the passenger side and helped her out of the car. His hand warmed her shoulders as he briefly pulled her toward him and guided her into the kitchen, where he pulled out a chair for her.

"How did you find me?"

"Something signaled up here." He tapped his forehead with his finger. "I just knew."

"Listen, I am so sorry—"

He cut her off. "No. That was my fault. All of it." He crossed his arms. "Doesn't matter. I'm going to help you find your niece. And don't worry. I won't take advantage again. That's a promise."

She wanted Peter out of her house, because his proximity was producing vertigo and palpitations, and not from their mental connection. She'd made a decision for her future, and he didn't fit into it.

Only now, she needed him to help her get to Quincy.

So she threw herself at him, then discarded him, and now she was going to use him. Who had become the monster now?

Guilt shredded her soul as she looked up into his face. The intensity of that stark, hungry expression rocked her back a step.

"You'll still help me?"

"Yes."

Fear clawed its way up her neck as she sat down. "Oh God, Quincy."

She put her head down on the table, trying to tamp down emotions and home in on the pictures tumbling around in her head. Peter sat down and combed his fingers through her hair, patient while her brain short-circuited. Where would this insanity stop? Would she eventually lose her mind? Yet with each pass of his hands over her scalp, a few extraneous images fell to the side and clarified what she was trying to see. The ache in her head receded under his caress.

"Don't stop." She lifted her head and stared into Peter's unfathomable black eyes.

"Don't stop what?"

"Touching me. It's helping me focus."

"You're not overwhelmed with the images of death anymore?"

"I'm overwhelmed with images of everything. I have no idea why, but I have more abilities than I did a few weeks ago."

"Fair enough. Let's see if more is better."

Turning her squarely to him, he kept one hand in contact with her scalp and guided her closer until their foreheads touched.

The rush of visions calmed.

Now, how could she gain clear sight into these images? Control them? How could she help Quincy?

"I've got an idea. Let me try blocking you, but I'm going to do something different. I will fish through my own mind," she said.

"What should I do?"

"Hold yourself back like you did before. But stay in physical contact with me no matter what. The connection between us seems to help."

As she leaned harder into his warm forehead, a quiet resolve washed over her. This time, she settled easily into the mental cocoon buffering her against the roaring waves of images. Only the images weren't as violent or as loud this time around. She felt Peter holding his consciousness back, and his control tamped down the cacophony of her own competing visions. Instead of moving forward into Peter's mind, as she had done before, she turned back into herself.

Every vision she had ever had in her entire life assaulted her all at once. Wide-eyed screams, people doubled over in pain, bodies crumpled in wrecks. When she pulled back, she dimly felt the increased pressure of Peter's strong hand on the back of her head as he maintained their connection.

Diving into the maelstrom, she nearly collapsed beneath the weight of death. Death of strangers, friends, loved ones. Death she had seen and tried to forget. She saw her college boyfriend's lifeless body in his crushed car, killed by a drunk driver, exactly as it had happened years ago.

Pain lanced through her gut as she watched her father wither away from the cancer that destroyed him, his skin stretched so thin that his bones seemed about to burst from his emaciated body. She heard his rattling wheeze as he smiled sadly and breathed his last. Tears ran unchecked over her cheeks, but she kept probing.

Quincy. Where was Quincy? Desperate, she searched her visions. There. The images from yesterday hung in front of her and she plucked at one like a silken string, unraveling it in front of her mind's eye.

Allison saw pine trees, a lake, a rushing creek, and familiar mountains.

Glass slipper, snow, up and down. Glass slipper, snow, up and down.

There was a bouncing rhythm to the images, punctuated by a child's whimper. Allison started to shake. Peter's vise-like grip on her head and shoulder clamped her face to his.

Focus on the slipper, focus on the slipper.

She slowed down the images. The man from the soccer field came into view, his crew cut and cruel face stark and clear, grinning. The scene bounced up and down. Snowy terrain moved by her as the man carried Quincy in his arms. Allison now saw the world through her niece's eyes. She concentrated harder.

The familiar creek tumbled down a narrow valley as Quincy traveled higher and higher into the mountains. One foot was bare, and on the other one, a glass slipper. The cold wind and snow cut into Quincy's exposed face and foot. Shivering, Allison delved deeper. This was happening right now. Allison was *there*.

The young girl's terror rose up like a suffocating tidal wave. Frantic, Allison pushed the emotion back, trying to regain control. She tried to compel her niece to look around, and shocked herself when the girl scanned the terrain.

Up high was a familiar snow-covered mountain, and at the base she saw a lake … and snow-covered cabins. Faint cross-country tracks led to the cabins.

She felt the man's hands dig into Quincy's body, and the bond faltered, then broke.

Like a bomb exploding in her sternum, the connection ceased, flinging her out of the vision backward into the present.

She screamed, head pounding, stars bursting in front of her eyes.

"Allie?" Peter shook her shoulders, causing a wave of nausea.

She dragged her attention back to him, waiting for the blurriness to clear.

"What happened?" He wiped the tears from her cheeks.

When he turned his head, she couldn't keep up with the motion and experienced another bout of vertigo. "Please. Hold still."

Her temples throbbed. She held down bile with sheer force of will.

"Are you okay?"

"No." She gasped. "Quincy. I was inside her mind."

"What did you say?" His vise-like grip dug into her upper arms.

"I got inside her head. You know how I kind of noodled into your brain when we first connected? Same thing, only I was right there, seeing through her eyes. The contact with you helped me focus."

"And?" Thank God he relaxed his clenched hands.

She struggled to put her recollection of the images together. Feeling the blood drain from her face, she said, "Aneroid Lake."

"What's that?"

Ignoring him, she stumbled to the laptop on the countertop and flipped it on. Her hand shook as she tried to click on the icon for the file she wanted. Opening the file, she found the photos from a winter hike a few years ago. One more click and she had it. The screen displayed Allison standing in front of a frozen lake, mountains rising behind her. Pine trees stippled the background. The shape of the lake, the mountain peaks, her vision of Quincy. Allison had been there.

"Oh God, that's where he's taken her. The man from the park. At least I think that's who it is. And I think that's where they're going."

She spun around and would have hit the floor if Peter hadn't grabbed under her arms. His tall frame enveloped her and held her upright until she could stand unaided. She could get used to fitting into his embrace. And that was the problem. She focused on the problem at hand.

"Do you know that for sure?" he asked.

When he rested his chin on top of her head, his voice rumbled through her skull. She shivered, recalling the cold snow and a bare foot. His warm hands smoothed over her back.

She buried her face in his chest. "No, I don't know that for sure. Who knows with the way my brain is changing? Maybe I'm losing my marbles." The hysterical, shrill laugh that bubbled out of her lips created a pitiful, alien sound.

He stared at her with an expression somewhere between disbelief and amazement. Perhaps he saw her cracking up and didn't know what to do.

God, she had always been in control in emergencies. Now look at her falling apart. And to top it off, she was willing to use this man's kindness and push the button of his own guilt, all to help her save Quincy's life.

He cleared his throat. "Well?"

She leaned back against his arms. "Let's go. I'm not 100 percent certain what I saw. Maybe it's stress or my own memories or wishful thinking. But I have to try something to help Quincy, and we're closer to the mountains. Even if it's a wild goose chase, at least we can try."

"Does it feel real?"

"Yes. As real as the images I saw when I touched you."

"Good enough for me."

She couldn't tell if he was merely placating her or truly believed what she told him. It didn't matter either way. "We need to get moving. If they're really where I think they are, it'll take a few hours to get to the lake."

"Not if I'm helping you. Let's go."

• • •

Allison donned her winter running gear and stuffed extra thermals and a jacket into a backpack along with plastic bags, heating packs, and extra socks for Quincy's cold feet. She checked to make sure a box of emergency waterproof matches was still in each backpack, and handed the extra pack to Peter to stuff with extra gear. In the garage, she grabbed her running snowshoes and a spare pair Sarah used when they hiked together.

They threw the equipment into the back of the Subaru, and Peter followed her directions to the highway. Soon, they had passed through the small towns of Enterprise and Joseph to reach Wallowa Lake State Park.

"Where to?" Peter drove too fast on the increasingly slippery roads. The sleet had changed over to wet snow and had started to build up on the road.

"Keep driving all the way to the trailhead. The road stops there." Doubt assailed her. Maybe she imagined all of the things she had seen, but the vision had seemed so real.

Drive faster.

He moved his hand from the steering wheel to cover hers. "If she's here, we'll find her."

"What if I'm wrong? This search is not logical," she said. "I should be in town helping to find her."

"What you saw about me was all true. I believe what you see." When he squeezed her hand, warmth coursed up her arm.

Ice covered most of Wallowa Lake. Mountains with thick pine trees rose steeply into low clouds on the south side of the lake. The state park was closed for the season, as the lack of people attested, but they continued anyway. Snow blanketed the chip-sealed road, and they followed a single set of tire tracks.

"Peter!" Allison pointed to a sedan parked near a brown Forest Service gate at the trailhead parking lot.

"Hold on." He parked near the other vehicle, jumped out of the car, and stopped short of the sedan, crouching to examine footprints fading in the light snow. When she joined him, he put a hand up, holding her back.

"One set of footprints, large, deep. They go past the gate and up that trail." He pointed to the trailhead sign. Light snow landed on his head, turning instantly into steam.

"What about Quincy?"

"I don't see anything."

Allison stepped up to the car, cupped her face, and held her breath, trying not to fog the window. She peered inside, pulse pounding. Under the front dashboard, something caught the light. Her heart thumped in her chest.

"Peter, come here." Her hands shook as she pointed. "What do you see?"

After a moment's contemplation, he answered, "Clear plastic slipper, child's size."

The muscle clenched in his jaw. His fury would've intimidated her, if she were the object of his rage.

She put a hand on his arm.

He spun back, his black stare boring through her. Acting on instinct, she reached out to him. As she connected with his corded forearm, he flinched, grabbing her wrist faster than the human eye could follow. For a split second, she feared he was going to break her arm.

Shaking his head, he snapped back from far away and looked right at her. He glanced down at his grip on her wrist and abruptly let go.

"I'm sorry. I was thinking about what I'd do if I had a daughter out there with this guy. I can imagine what Bryce is going through."

"We have to get to Quincy."

They opened the back of Allison's car, pulling out backpacks and gear. Peter put his hands on her shoulders. "You shouldn't go. It's too dangerous. Besides, I can move faster on my own."

Anger flared, and she shrugged his hands off. "I have the radar system, remember?"

"I don't want you in danger." He ran a hand through his dark hair.

She snapped the snowshoes on over her boots and shoved a yarn hat over her hair. "Not your decision." Flipping the backpack over her shoulder, she started up the trail, not caring if he followed, but confident that he would.

Chapter 16

Peter kept up with Allie's light jog. As they climbed higher up East Fork Trail, the snow underfoot thickened and pine tree branches above sagged with the constant snowfall. Little puffs of vapor punctuated her every snowshoed step and hiking pole placement.

He had the perfect view of her rounded backside and toned legs encased in thick running tights. If only those legs were wrapped around his waist as he leaned over to kiss her ... his mutinous groin tightened at the fantasy.

When she stopped abruptly, he almost ran into her.

She let out a quick breath. "Are you all right?"

"Fine, you?"

Hell, he had no business thinking about her as if they had a future. For her safety and that of her family, he needed to exit her life after they found Quincy and he dealt with the minion. No matter how intoxicating Allison La Croix was, he couldn't stick around and bring more evil into her world. He'd suppress his desires, to keep her safe.

Her emerald eyes sparkled as the snow fell around them. "Good. Just needed a quick drink."

While she rested, he calculated many scenarios about what awaited them at the end of the trail. Adrenaline zipped through his veins, making the muscles in his arms and legs jump. Damn this waiting game. How the hell was he going to get a young girl out of a kidnapper's hands? If that guy had a similar makeup as Peter, killing the man wouldn't be easy. In fact, it might be impossible, if they were too evenly matched. And if the man had an advantage? Peter would have to slow the man down, stay alive himself, keep Allie safe, and save Quincy. No way could he accomplish all of those tasks. Something would have to give, but what?

He scowled up at the cloudy midday sky as he calculated the hours of daylight left. Catching a glimpse of her luminous face, pink in the cold air, he couldn't formulate a plan of attack in his mind. He couldn't stop staring at her full lips, set in a grim line. He had to focus on getting Quincy, but damn it, Allie's soft skin captured his attention.

When she swung the backpack around and pulled out a water bottle, the vision of her lips on the container nearly ruined him. Before he registered the action, he ran his thumb over his bottom lip.

He curled his hand into a fist and shoved it into his jeans pocket. "Any more images of Quincy?"

"Not specifically, only flickers. I think we're heading in the right direction. It feels right." She motioned with a gloved hand toward the toboggan on her head. "And even with the snow falling, I can still see indentions from his footprints."

He knelt and touched a deep footprint. "He didn't have snowshoes on. It might take him a little longer to cover the same terrain."

"Is it slower even for someone like you?" At Peter's nod, she continued. "He's post-holing with every step, so it's got to take effort to keep hiking the trail. It'll get worse the higher we go; steep switchbacks begin twenty yards or so up the trail."

"How much farther are we talking about total?"

She squinted at the cloud-covered mountains. "About three more miles. It's a steep trail. We'll go up another 2,000 feet in elevation. I'm guessing the snow will be way deeper up there."

"Why don't I help you a little?"

"Pardon?"

Her deep green gaze took his breath away. *Concentrate.*

"I can carry you for a while." At her scowl, he put his hands up, palms to her. "Not that you're not making great time. You're doing fine."

"But?"

"Well, I don't really get … tired. I can cover terrain more quickly than you'd be able to by yourself. You can rest and focus on Quincy."

She eyed the trail. "Well, if it's not going to hurt you or wear you out … "

"I promise. The side effect of my condition is that I'm like a freakish Energizer bunny."

Her quick smile lit up her entire face. He could get used to making her smile like that forever. If he had the right forever, that is.

She replaced her bottle in the backpack and zipped it up. "Okay, that makes sense. The sooner we get up there, the better. So, how … ?"

"Let's try piggyback. I can keep my hands free and use your poles to move faster." He turned his backpack around to wear it on his chest. Motioning toward the dangerously tapered tails of her snowshoes, he said, "Maybe you should take those off? I might be semi-dead, but I'm still a guy and those will be much too close for comfort."

She blushed red and removed and stowed her snowshoes.

He crouched as she stepped up behind him. Awkward in the snow, she jumped, and he caught her under her thighs and lifted, settling her on his hipbones. She wriggled to get situated, and he clamped his jaw down tightly as she nestled into the small of his back.

"All set?" he ground out hoarsely. Maybe this arrangement was a bad decision.

She looped one arm over his shoulder and the other under his armpit and laced her gloved fingers together. She locked her feet at his waist. "Yes."

Peter picked up her poles and headed up the trail. Whether it was the mission, the crisp air, or the beautiful woman attached to his back, Peter didn't know what gave him the spring in his step as he bounded up the switchbacks.

• • •

Allison conceded this was a great idea. Peter's smooth, strong gait ate up the trail. The corded muscles of his upper butt and thighs bunched with each step, doing delightful things to the areas of her body pressed against him.

Thank God for his indefatigable strength. Although she was no slouch hiking on snowshoes, they were moving twice as fast at his pace. The creek disappeared into a ravine as they increased elevation. Once the trail bordered the creek again, they'd almost be at Aneroid Lake, in an hour or so.

But even if her crazy ability led them to Quincy, what next? Nothing. Peter had his obligation to kill criminals for hundreds more years. She'd made her decision clear. They had no future together. But that didn't mean she couldn't enjoy these fleeting moments of closeness before they parted. She'd come to rely on his steady faith in her gift, his assurance that they could do the impossible and rescue Quincy while getting out of this mess alive.

With a sigh, she rested her cheek on the back of his neck, absorbing the heat radiating out from his skin. Her lips grazed his hairline.

"Allie, you need to stop that." His voice reverberated through her body.

"It's helping me focus on Quincy."

"Yes, but *my* focus deserts me every time you breathe there."

When she nuzzled right behind his ear, she felt the shudder pass through him. "You want me to stop?"

"Never," he said.

They crested the hill and rejoined the creek.

She breathed in his spicy, warm scent. The crunch of his snowshoes and the distant rushing creek created a calming sound. Lulled by his warmth and his steady stride, she kept her face pressed to his neck and let her mind wander.

The connection lacked strength, but Allison managed to get back into her niece's thoughts. Through Quincy's eyes, Allison saw gray snow and a dark hole in the mountainside. She sobbed in terror as she was dragged into the darkness. The feedback from Quincy's exhaustion crept into Allison's arms, and she lost all of her strength.

Peter stopped and grabbed her sagging legs. "What is it?"

As he boosted her back up, she forced herself to hold on again. "I'm not sure. Something's going on with Quincy. It's dark." She shook her head, trying to clear the fuzzy feeling. "Keep going, please, if you're not too tired."

"Not at all." He picked up the pace, panting a bit as his efficient strides moved them up the trail.

After a half hour, they crested another hill, and the terrain opened up into a wider valley where the creek, now a small stream, cut through a snowfield. Dotted throughout the valley were lodgepole pine trees. Low clouds hid the timberline and the mountaintops. A frozen lake came into view.

At the edge of the lake, the tracks stopped, and then went in opposite directions.

Peter stopped and helped Allison down. Without his warmth, she was lost, alone. The difficulty focusing must be due to fatigue. She dragged her attention to the tracks.

"What do you think?" he asked.

To the south, the tracks circled the lake beneath a slope of granite. The other set entered a stand of trees and appeared to be moving toward the open area at the far side of the lake.

He frowned. "Is he throwing us off? Playing games?"

She took off her glove. Grasping his warm hand, she focused on Quincy and felt a pull toward the north. "That way." She nodded in the direction of the path through the trees.

Both on snowshoes now, they hiked through the trees as the snow fell. Arriving at the back of the lake, she spied a few small cabins on the hillside. She also felt hidden eyes on her.

"What's that?" He pointed to a circular wooden structure.

"That's a yurt. This is a small parcel carved out of Forest Service land from years ago when folks would pack horses up here to spend their summers."

"Is Quincy in one of the cabins?"

Allison concentrated. "No, I don't think so, even though there are tracks to almost all of the cabins."

"Putting us off the scent again?"

"Yes, but how does he know we're following him?"

• • •

Peter stopped cold in his tracks.

You must be getting close to being free. They threw the whole kit and caboodle at Barnaby before he finished his contract.

"What is it, Peter?"

He couldn't meet her eyes. "The man who took Quincy knew we would come up here."

"How?"

Dread sucker-punched him in the stomach. "Your power. He knows about it. Hell, that means Jerahmeel knows about it, too. Not good."

"Aren't you supposed to kill this guy?"

"Maybe. What I do know is that it's me he's ultimately after."

"So that leaves me off the hook, right?"

He rubbed his jaw. "No. You're in grave danger. You're the collateral damage, the leverage. Oh, hell."

"Why?"

Damn her trusting green eyes watching him like he would keep her safe. She had no idea. He had no idea if he even possessed enough strength to get her out of here alive before the minion attacked.

"This whole mess has to do with my contract ending. With the Meaningful Kill."

"I don't understand."

Deep, unrelenting fear doused him awake as surely as a bucket of ice water. This situation was a deadly endgame, and not for Peter. "They're going to try to destroy anything dear to me, to prevent me from completing the contract."

"But completing the contract, that's good, right?"

At the impossible hope in her eyes, he had an overwhelming urge to kiss her pink nose. Then he wanted to shake her so she would understand the mortal danger she was in.

"Not if other people get hurt. He knew about your power. He knew you would lead me here. You have to leave. Now."

She planted the poles and shot him an icy green glare. "I'm not leaving Quincy."

He raked his hand through his hair. Never had he felt this helpless as a man, not even when Claire lay in the iron lung.

"Allie, I don't know if I can beat this guy. I might not be able to keep you alive. This is serious."

Her chin jutted out. *Uh oh.* "I agree this is serious. I will find Quincy—with or without you."

This brave, selfless woman would be the death of him. He had to save Quincy, destroy the minion, and keep Allie from being annihilated—all at the same time. How the hell could he pull this off? But if her crossed arms were any indication, he had no choice but to move forward.

He pointed up the frozen lakeshore. "Put your radar on. Let's find Quincy and maybe we can sneak out of here."

Cold realization steadied his churning thoughts until he reached a state of calm, lethal focus. He couldn't destroy the minion.

But he could sacrifice himself for Allie. Hell. He set his jaw and followed her up the mountainside, every movement and every thought fixed on the task at hand.

Hiking past the cabins, Allie briefly stopped in front of each one with her hands outstretched, checking for Quincy. She motioned for them to continue onward.

Peter compulsively scanned the surrounding area, his nerves stretched taut. For the second time today, he nearly ran into Allie as she stopped short. The tracks traveled up a hillside and entered a dense stand of trees.

He didn't like this situation one bit. "I'm in front."

"Not arguing with you there." She followed him, bending into the incline.

All he could hear was Allie's light breath and the crunch of snow under the snowshoes as they skirted a boulder field. Soon, the trees thinned out and the tracks led into a small clearing.

Peter's internal alarm rang like a loud klaxon in his head. *Where is the minion, damn it?*

On the hillside he spied an old mine entrance with snow disturbed in front of it.

Peter's body tensed at a flicker of movement out of the corner of his eye.

Strolling down the snowy slope was the stocky man from the park: the minion.

Allie gasped.

Peter stepped in front of her.

The guy grinned. Snow sizzled as it landed on the minion's head.

"Hello, Mr. Blackstone." Tense, manic lines formed at the corners of the minion's bloodshot eyes.

Peter put an arm back to keep Allie behind him. "I believe you have me at a disadvantage."

He studied the minion and scanned the surrounding area, every sense dedicated to his mission. Where was Quincy?

"My name's Anton. I'm an associate of our big boss, Jerahmeel." He snickered for a minute. "Ah, hello, my beautiful pretty pretty."

When Anton leered at Allie, only Peter's desire to protect her kept him from rushing at the man. If he stepped away, she'd be too exposed. Anton would have to go through Peter to get to her.

Anton tapped an eyebrow. "Lovely meeting you the other day." His harsh, barking laugh raked through the cold air.

"Where's Quincy?"

"That delectable little girl?" Anton licked his dry lips.

"What have you done to her?" Peter's gut turned to ice.

"I made a new friend. You want to see?"

"She's an innocent. Leave her out of this."

"Oh, Petey, this has nothing to do with that sweet child. Or that yummy, scrummy lady there." He inclined his head toward Allie, who, to her credit, had moved to stand tall at Peter's side. "Although your mortal girlfriend is going to be a tasty treat. Then maybe I'll take care of that little girl, too."

He licked his lips and gestured toward the mine opening.

"You son of a bitch!" Peter roared. "Leave them out of this. Step aside, Anton."

Anton cast an eerie, feral smile at Allie. "Wouldn't you like to see the little girly girly?" He scratched at his head.

Allie's voice quivered. "Please let me go to her."

He tapped his eyebrow again and giggled, a high-pitched, dry squeal. "Of course. But you have to get around me first."

His hollow laugh bounced off the snowy hillside, the reverberation grating on Peter's nerves. Allie staggered forward a step, holding her head. When she looked up at Peter, the pain was etched on her fine features. To hell with his control. He would tear the minion's arms from his sockets and enjoy the pop of bone separating from sinew. To hell with Peter's life.

He hurled himself at the minion, flying across the open space. With a sickening crunch of bone impacting bone, they rolled to the ground, locked together. Peter's snowshoes broke and flew off. Maneuvering Anton away from the mine entrance, Peter punched him in the jaw repeatedly, snapping his head back. The minion spit out teeth.

Peter had to buy time for Allie to rescue Quincy. He needed to distract or disable the minion. Neither action would be easy.

As he scrambled to his feet, Anton struck back, shattering Peter's rib with a deep snap.

Peter fought a wave of nausea as the rib shifted and knitted back together within seconds. He held his breath, bracing himself against the agony. Tasting blood, he recovered enough to return a punch and kick combination that staggered Anton. The minion shook his head and ran at Peter, bellowing like an enraged bull.

He hit Peter with enough force to hurl him down into the pine trees. More bones cracked. The snowy world inverted as Peter scraped down the trunk and fell headfirst into a drift of snow. His vision blurred, leaving only a smear of white with black specks flitting across. It would take a minute to see again. Hell, he didn't have a minute.

Digging out of the snow, he squinted against his throbbing headache and willed the healing to go faster. One dark shape moved toward the opening of the mine.

Allie? Or Anton?

Chapter 17

With the men locked in vicious battle, Allison crept around the far edge of the clearing, approaching the mine entrance from the side. A rope lay coiled at the opening of the mine; a length disappeared into the mouth of the tunnel.

Staying low, she crouched just inside the entrance, probing the tunnel with her mind. As she slipped off her snowshoes, Quincy's aura pinged weakly back to her, almost like sonar. Allison pulled her backpack around and fished out a flashlight. Looping the strap over her wrist, she clicked it on but saw only a small tunnel vanishing into darkness.

At that moment, Anton shot her a bloody grin from across the clearing, despite Peter's blows. "What do we have here? Lovely, lovely intruder."

In a whoosh of air Anton hurled Peter into the trees on the other side of the clearing. Peter landed with a sickening crunch of bone and branches that she could hear, even at this distance. He didn't move.

Oh God.

She had to get Quincy.

Anton stalked toward the mine entrance.

Terror driving her, she dove into the tunnel and hunched down, half running, half crawling into the dusty mine. Supporting timbers flashed by. She expected to see Anton right behind her. But when she looked back, he remained at the entrance. Her flashlight's beam bounced off his sadistic leer, backlit by the snowy terrain behind him.

He had the rope in his hand.

"Bye-bye, pretty pretty." He pulled the cord as Peter collided with him, knocking Anton away from the entrance.

She heard a rumble above her as her flashlight beam caught a bare foot ahead in the tunnel. Quincy!

Rocks crashed down around them.

Crouching, she scooped up the limp girl. Swinging the flashlight around, she desperately searched for safety.

There, a tiny niche next to a supporting beam. As she squeezed herself and Quincy into the space, the tunnel collapsed. Rocks banged off her back and head as she cradled Quincy, shielding her niece as the entire world fell down around them.

Allison cried out as a rock glanced off her leg, and Quincy whimpered and shifted. She held her niece tighter as the deep, deafening rumbling continued. Minutes passed.

A dusty, ominous silence descended in the pitch-black.

• • •

Peter struggled to his feet and crossed the clearing. As he approached the mine entrance, Anton yelled into the black hole and pulled the cord. A loud rumbling and a plume of black dust erupted.

Allie.

Hell. She's in there.

Between one blink and the next, Pater bent the minion beneath more vicious blows. Anton wheezed and stumbled backward. Peter refused to stop, even though he'd eventually wear out, despite his super strength. With every kick and punch, fear and fury mixed into an all-consuming, explosive compound inside Peter's mind. He tried to destroy the minion with his bare hands, his only goal to drive the man away from the mine entrance. He threw Anton into the boulder field, the minion's eerie screams bouncing off the snowy landscape.

Slower now and favoring one leg, Anton returned. Blood flowed from his damaged nose. One limp arm hung at his side. The minion charged, frothing and yelling.

Honing his rage, fear, and strength into a lethal point of convergence, a state of surreal calm came over Peter. This was it. He pulled the knife from his ankle holster. Anton stopped short and rocked back on his heels.

"You can't use that on me," he said, eyes bulging.

"And why not?" Peter shook with fury.

Every minute he had to deal with Anton was a minute Allie might not have.

Bloody spittle formed at the corners of Anton's mouth. "The rules. We can't use the blades on each other."

"Does it appear that I care about rules?"

He pointed at the black cloud of dust drifting out of the mine, then struck without warning, backing Anton down the slope with vicious slices. When he pierced Anton's side with the blade, the minion howled.

"You can't do that!" Anton stared in horror as dark blood spread over his shirt.

"Of course I can," Peter said calmly. "And I intend to destroy you with it."

He lunged, grazing the man's leg. Blood spurted. Anton screamed in pain as Peter's knife began to glow.

"Oh, Anton, she's hungry for you," Peter crooned, brandishing the blade.

Blinded by desire to fill the knife with prey's blood, Peter struck with a killing blow, but Anton turned at the last moment. The luminescent knife glanced off the minion's chest wall, filleting clothing and a dinner plate-sized chunk of flesh. Dark blood pulsed out of the wound, melting the snow beneath the steaming piece of minion meat.

Shrieking with the force of a train whistle, the minion hit Peter hard enough to knock him to his knees and cloud his vision again before the minion sprinted down the hillside. Peter saw him as a bloody blur, skirting the lake and dodging onto the return trail down the mountain. Anton left a path of blood in his wake, visible even from where Peter sprawled.

Peter staggered to his feet and shook his head again, clearing it. Anton wouldn't win the day today, but the minion would heal and gather his strength. He'd be back. *May you get an infection and gangrene and rot.* Too bad that wasn't possible.

Every nerve in his body strained to finish the kill. But with the knife still glowing with unfulfilled hunger, Peter dragged his base desires back to the present priority.

Scrambling across the trampled, bloody snow to the entrance of the mine, he peered inside. Dust and rocks sealed the mine access five feet into the entrance. Peter's blood ran cold. Allie was down there. Trapped. Possibly hurt. Or dead.

"Allie!" he yelled.

Only rock-solid silence answered him.

· · ·

In the heavy blackness, Allison took stock of her situation. She slowed her panicked breathing and took a slow, deep inhalation. Mistake. She choked on the dusty air.

By some miracle, the flashlight still dangled from her wrist. Praying it would work, she clicked it on, the LED glow illuminating her tomb.

Her right leg was buried under a foot of rubble. The timber she had huddled against held the worst rock fall away from them, but rock encased them. There wasn't a whisper of air movement. No sound met her ears except for her harsh breathing and Quincy's whimper.

Unwrapping her left arm from the backpack, she chafed Quincy's arms, alarmed at how cold her niece was.

"Mmmph, Mommy?" the girl mumbled.

Her heart twisted. "No sweetie, it's Auntie Al."

"Auntie Al?" Quincy started crying and turned to wrap her arms around Allison's neck.

She patted Quincy's back and murmured reassurances, rocking her. The movement hurt her leg, but she ignored it.

"Let me see you, sweetie." Allison turned her flashlight at a shivering Quincy. Her niece's face was caked with dust, lined with tear streaks, but there was no apparent head injury. She ran both hands over the girl's head, arms, chest, and legs. Quincy's feet were icy.

"I'm cold."

"I know, sweetie. Let's get you warmed up."

Allison pulled on her own leg, but it wouldn't move. She shifted rocks and, gritting her teeth against the pain, yanked her leg out from the rubble. Several chunks of rock and dirt released from the ceiling. If she moved too much, they'd be crushed for sure.

Quincy's pale face floated before her in the flashlight's yellow glow. "I'm hungry, too."

"I bet you are." She fished in her backpack for supplies. "First of all, we'll warm up those tootsies."

Working in the limited space, Allison pulled out hand warmers and broke them open, shaking vigorously to activate the iron oxide and charcoal. Warmth emanated from the packets, and she placed them against Quincy's feet, putting a plastic bag and a sock on top of each one.

Quincy giggled. "That's silly, a plastic bag."

"Yep, you're a bag lady now."

Allison crossed her eyes and stuck out her tongue, trying to distract Quincy from her discomfort. She next stripped off Quincy's thin Cinderella dress and pulled on two thermal tops and bottoms, knotting the excess material at the hems. She added a woolen cap and tied the flaps under Quincy's chin.

"Better?" At her nod, Allison asked, "Want a snack?"

Quincy licked her dry lips as Allison handed her niece a water bottle.

"Drink first. It's important."

After they both had some water, Allison capped the bottle and replaced it in the backpack. She produced a granola bar and was pleased when Quincy finished it.

"How do we get out?" Quincy asked, lower lip quivering.

"Don't worry. Mr. Peter will help us. The best thing to do is rest."

For all she knew, he wasn't even alive. Her breaths started to come quicker, and Allison fought to maintain control. Desperation gripped her, riding the rapid heart rate pounding in her chest. Finally, she forced herself to take a calming breath as she relaxed her tense muscles. When she settled Quincy into her lap, the girl tucked her head into Allison's chest and fell fast asleep.

After taking stock of her situation, the prognosis was grim. If he was alive, she had no idea if even someone as strong as Peter could unbury them without large machinery. How much oxygen remained in the pocket of rubble?

And the mine's stability? Questionable at best. Simply moving her leg caused another small rock fall. She could only imagine what digging under the ceiling would do. They'd be buried before anyone could get to them.

She had one more bottle of water and three more granola bars. That wouldn't last long. No one knew they were at this particular lake, in this mine. No one except for Peter, and Anton may have killed him.

So no one was coming.

Oh God. She and her niece were going to slowly die here in this hole, and Allison couldn't do anything about it. Terror made her lightheaded. Or maybe it was the lack of oxygen, which she admitted was becoming a very real threat now.

It took twice the effort to draw in enough air. Her chest burned and her fingertips started to tingle.

Try to relax.

The only thing left to do was attempt to connect with Peter. Her freakish, evolving powers had to be good for something, right?

Resting her head against the cold wall, she closed her eyes and forced her numb mind to reach back through the rubble into the clearing. Again, like sonar, she sensed the pain and rage boiling in Peter's head. At least he was still alive. Maybe her gift could save them now.

Maybe.

She tried to reach out to get him to notice her.

How do I do that? Knock?

She pulled at the neckline of her shirt, trying to gulp a breath. She had trouble concentrating.

Pushing her thoughts as hard as she could, she tried to send him a message. Suddenly, their connection snapped into place, like two opposite magnet poles clicking into each other. He was right there in her mind. With the last of her depleted reserves, she pushed her message to him.

"Help me."

She passed out in the frigid, pitch-black tomb.

Chapter 18

"Allie?" he said aloud and in his mind.

Silence.

Nothing remained of her in his consciousness. His heart pounded in his chest. Time had run out.

He ran back across the clearing and grabbed the backpack he'd dropped before fighting Anton. Pulling out a flashlight, he set it at the entrance of the mineshaft. The waning late afternoon light and flashlight glow gave him enough visibility to work. He clawed at the rubble, hurling rocks out of the mine at a rate no mortal could match. Every few minutes a section of roof collapsed on him, the stones banging off his back and head, but grimly, he kept digging.

He reached out with his mind and touched ... nothing. Cold sweat rolled down his face. How much rock did he have to move? How much time did he have?

Get to Allie.

She had to be alive. Even if he couldn't be with her, at least he would know she lived. That would be enough.

He dug faster.

The knife on his leg pulsed with hungry heat, its appetite whetted but not yet slaked. Damn it, he still had to deal with Anton, but not now. Ignoring the knife's pull, Peter kept digging, his scratched hands healing almost as quickly as he injured them.

The minutes crept by. He kept going. His whole existence boiled down to getting these two people free from the hell he had caused. Rock by flung rock, he inched deeper into the mine, tunneling into the rubble.

Finally, he removed a large rock and stopped. There was nothing behind it. Grabbing the flashlight, he shone it into blackness. Turning the beam downward he saw a familiar leg and boot.

"Allie?" When there was no response, his gut clenched. "Allie?" he called louder, his voice absorbed by the small space where she lay.

Stale, lifeless air returned through the hole he'd created in the rubble.

Desperate to reach her, he shoved away more rocks. Old supporting timbers bowed downward. How much time did he have before the ceiling came down?

Almost there. He had a small opening in the wall now and heard a paroxysmal cough and frantic wheeze.

"Allie?"

"Peter?" she panted.

He heard movement on the other side of the wall and a flashlight beam pierced the darkness.

When he peered into the black hole, her dirt-covered face and glassy eyes staring back at him were the most beautiful sight he'd ever seen. Her chest heaved as she gulped fresh air. Quincy's limp form lay in her arms.

"Peter, get her out of here!" She rose up, yelping as dirt and rocks poured down over her shoulders.

"Don't move."

Gingerly, he removed a few more rocks, making room for the girl. His hands shook as he forced himself to work carefully. But he had to hurry. The whole ceiling was about to collapse. Black thoughts of what he wanted to do with Anton welled up again.

Focus.

"Can you push Quincy up to me? Go slowly," he called to Allie.

She nudged Quincy until the girl woke up and whimpered.

"It's okay, honey. Mr. Peter is here to help us. I need you to lift your arms and hold his hands, please."

He grasped the girl's forearms and guided her out of the hole. Pulling Quincy free, he rolled back onto several sharp rocks, wincing as he bore the brunt of the impact. He cradled her in his arms, and, in a crouch, scrambled out of the tunnel, depositing the crying girl in the trampled snow outside the mine entrance.

A timber creaked ominously as he raced back down the mine. He had to get Allie out of here. Now.

Reaching the hole in the rock, he called, "Can you get to me?"

She coughed. "Maybe, but if I force myself through a small space, it'll collapse."

Her tight, high-pitched voice conveyed every bit of anxiety he also felt.

Working even faster than he could register the movements, he shifted more material out of the way. Additional creaks preceded more falling dirt.

"Come on, Allie." He held his hands out, willing her to move faster.

Emerging from the darkness, her slim hand made contact with his, and the jolt of mixed terror and joy stunned him. He pulled until he grasped beneath her arms.

With an ominous rumble, the wooden beams above them shuddered.

Heart thudding, Peter braced his feet and heaved her out through the narrow passage, trying to ignore her cries when she landed on the rocks. A heavy ceiling timber came loose, barely missing her.

Peter half ran, half crawled up the tunnel, dragging Allie behind him as rocks rained down. He burst from the mine, flinging Allie onto the snow as the remainder of the supports failed, sealing the tunnel behind them in a cloud of black dust.

Allie sprawled on the snowy ground, coughing, struggling for air. Snow fell on her dirt-covered skin, making clean dots where each new snowflake landed. He could still make out her face as twilight faded to evening.

Peter crouched over her. "Are you hurt?"

He pushed the tangled hair away from her face. She'd lost her hat in the mine collapse.

"Quincy?" She sobbed for air.

"Auntie Al?" came the girl's high voice a few feet away. "I'm cold."

"Oh, sweetie." Allie sat up and reached out shaking arms for her niece, hugging her. "We'll get you warm."

Allie's flashlight was still attached to her arm. With a blank expression, she clicked it on to reveal thickly falling snow, now driven by a harsh wind.

Clinging to each other, both she and Quincy started to shiver.

He knelt in the snow next to them. "We've got to get you two dried off and warm. What about going down the mountain?"

Allie shook her head. "Quincy can't survive several more hours of pure exposure without getting warmed up first. She's already hypothermic and her clothes are wet. And my backpack with the extra heating packs is back there." She gestured toward the sealed mine entrance.

"How about one of those cabins?"

"That's the safest option, at least until it's light out again. We also have only one set of snowshoes now."

He helped her to stand and then picked up a shivering Quincy. He opened his jacket to conduct some of his heat into the girl's body. Quincy's teeth chattered next to his chest.

Handing Allie his pair of snowshoes, he said, "Lead the way to the cabins."

She buckled them on and slung his backpack over her shoulder. "We'll go back through the trees where we came in and then angle down toward the lake. Hopefully, we will reach a cabin."

• • •

Holding the flashlight, Allison led the way, trying to move in what she guessed was the right direction. The snowfall had thickened to the point where the beam wouldn't penetrate more than a few feet in front of them. The tracks from their hike up the hill earlier today had all but vanished.

Adrenaline draining away, she fought to put one foot in front of the other. Peter followed close behind with an ominously silent Quincy in his arms. She needed to get her niece warmed up.

What if Anton comes back?

She refused to consider that possibility for now.

Reaching the boulder field, she headed directly downhill, hearing the faint sounds of the stream, muffled in the falling snow.

"Do you know where we are?" Peter asked.

She projected more confidence than she felt. "This should be the stream that leads to the lake. As long as we're slightly uphill from it, we should run into at least one of the cabins. If not, we can double back a little higher on the hill."

Panic kept her weary eyes open now. So tired. Her joints ached from being buried alive. But at least they were free of the mine. What if they hadn't arrived in time, or Anton had decided to bury Quincy alone? Allison shuddered.

As desperate as she was to find shelter, she kept imagining cabins rising out of the darkness. When a structure appeared in front of her, she stopped and stared mutely, not sure if it was real.

"Allie? What's that?"

"I thought I dreamt it," she whispered. "I think it's the outdoor club's hiking hut."

At the base of the compact wooden yurt, a snowdrift blocked the door. Wordlessly handing Quincy to Allison, Peter dug out the door with his bare hands. He worked faster than Allison could follow, but she kept the light trained on the door so he could see. She managed to remain standing and to hold on to Quincy, although exhaustion turned her arms and legs to Jell-O.

Once he had the door cleared, he chopped the doorknob with his hand, breaking the latch. Yanking the door open, he motioned them inside, taking Quincy back as Allison removed the snowshoes and stumbled into the building.

The hut contained four low wooden platforms for hikers' sleeping bags, a small wooden table, and a central stove, its metal pipe exiting through the center of the roof. A bucket of kindling sat next to the stove. Right about now, the cabin looked luxurious and cozy to Allison.

Relief, exhaustion, and cold all settled on her shoulders and she collapsed clumsily onto the floor. Moving quickly, Peter lowered Quincy to her, then laid the dry tinder in the stove and dismantled the table and two sleeping pallets into small pieces. After lighting one of the waterproof matches from a box she had insisted on placing in each of their packs, on the second strike, he cupped his hand around the flame until a piece of kindling caught.

She could already imagine the heat even though it would take much more time to reach her. Quincy murmured in her arms, the shivers stopping. It was a bad progression of symptoms. The girl needed fluids and to warm up. Soon.

Stacking pieces of the table on the fire, Peter closed the stove door and laid another pile next to it. "Use these to keep feeding the fire. Get it really stoked. I'm going to get more wood so we can get this place as warm as possible."

Stabbing fear paralyzed her for a split second and she blurted out, "Please don't go far."

He ran his rough hand over her cheek, his eyes black in the dim light. "I'll stay close. I promise."

She nodded blankly as Peter exited the yurt. The only light came from the small windows in the flickering stove. Outside the building, cracks and explosions reverberated through the walls of the hut.

After a time, Allison laid Quincy on the cold floor and opened the stove, shoving in several more pieces of wood. She sat as close as she dared with Quincy, turning her niece so the snow-dampened seat of Quincy's pants could dry. She debated stripping off the child's clothes, but decided against it. The room remained much too chilly.

She checked the girl's pulse. Steady but too rapid. When she pinched her niece's skin, it remained tented. Quincy was exhausted, hypothermic, and dehydrated. Allison couldn't rouse her to drink anything.

When Allison's stomach growled, she pulled out two granola bars and washed them down with the water. Instead of her gaining more energy, lethargy oozed through every pore of her body. She'd dozed off when the door swung open with a blast of cold air, startling her.

Peter held a large bundle of broken wood. He dumped his load of branches next to the flickering stove and pushed the yurt door closed.

• • •

"It's already warmer in here," he said.

Allie's haunted eyes drilled into him.

She put her hand on the girl's head. "Big improvement. But we need to get out of here at first light. Quincy needs medical care. What time is it?"

He glanced at his watch. "Pushing midnight. We can leave in six hours when there's enough light to safely hike back down. In the meantime, let's get you two more comfortable."

Yanking one of the remaining sleeping pallets out of the wall, he dragged it in front of the stove.

Allie eased Quincy onto the pallet. Her niece's dust-covered face had turned rosier, but the girl didn't wake up with the movement. Allie stood, her shoulders slumped, and turned into Peter's open arms. She sagged into his chest, shaking with sobs.

He swallowed a lump in his throat and cradled her, careful of her bruised body. He brushed away the tears, kissed her forehead, and tucked her back into the shelter of his arms. Resting his chin on the crown of her head, fury and possessiveness began to blend into his emotions. He needed her. He didn't want to let her go. But he couldn't stay with her and expose this woman to more evil.

"Why?" she asked, her voice muffled by his shirt.

Guilt pierced his heart. He damn well knew the answer and would take ownership of this mess. "I'm the reason you and Quincy got hurt. It's my fault."

"I don't understand."

Peter ran his fingers over the soft skin of her neck. "You were right before. Anton *is* someone like me. Only he's worse. His job is to keep me from finishing my contract." Her lithe frame fit perfectly against his, trusting him. He didn't deserve this woman.

"Okay, but why did he have to hurt Quincy?"

The anger behind her question was justified.

"When our kind get close to finishing their contracts, Jerahmeel throws everything at us to make it difficult to obtain the Meaningful Kill. Jerahmeel wants to hurt anyone I care about, shut down my motivation to try and break the contract. It may be that Anton is my Meaningful Kill. By finding a way to finish him off, I could be done killing forever."

She burrowed deeper into his chest. "How hard would that be? Killing him?"

"Very. He's exceptionally strong. I had to cheat to slow him down. But it's not impossible to kill him."

"That would be a good thing, getting out of your contract. Right?"

"Not for Jerahmeel. He needs as many of us as possible killing for him to maintain his supply of power. When one of us drops out, it reduces his food source. And his energy."

"But if you finish the contract, that would be good for you, right?"

"Yes. Then I could have a normal life, like a normal man. And perhaps spend it with one person." He stared down at her. "But only if I can finish my contract."

"Oh," she said softly.

He lowered his mouth to her lips and kissed her tenderly, and then wrapped her back up in his arms. She leaned against him.

"You need to rest."

"But Anton—"

"He won't get to you tonight. I'll be right here, I promise." He could at least do this one thing.

He helped her to the pallet, easing her onto her side next to Quincy. Peter put more wood in the stove, increasing the heat. He sat down on the floor and rested his hands on her head and hip, determined to maintain contact. Turning awkwardly, he kept his eyes on the door and held silent guard over Allie and her niece.

Chapter 19

The morning arrived cold and windy. Peter had spent the entire night vigilant, refusing to doze off. Anton was still out there, injured but alive. He would see the minion again, no question, but where and when?

The knife on his leg pulsed with thirsty anticipation.

Flat, gray light illuminated the yurt's windows. He rocked Allie's hip to wake her. She rolled over, her face streaked with dried tear tracks and dirt, circles under her eyes, hair knotted and tousled. Peter had never seen anyone more lovely.

He brushed the hair off her forehead. "Time to go."

She sat up, rubbing her face, and turned to Quincy, who was more difficult to rouse. The grumpy six-year-old swatted weakly at her aunt's hands and rolled back over.

"Let's go. She'll wake up out there. I hope."

Thankfully, the snow had diminished to flurries. "Ready to get down the mountain?"

"Yes, the sooner the better."

Allie donned her snowshoes and took off into the crisp morning air. They would make better time going back down.

Carrying the backpack and Quincy, he followed over the fresh snow. How did Allie keep going? She had to be exhausted.

Without snowshoes, he post-holed every step. He might be strong, but deep snow slowed even him down. His muscles ached, an unusual sensation. His arms full with Quincy, he concentrated on his foot placement.

A smear of fresh blood on a tree trunk near the outlet of Aneroid Lake reminded him to stay alert. Anton could be anywhere. Although he hoped the man had gone to ground to lick his wounds, no one was safe as long as that monster walked this Earth.

Quincy had finally woken up and Allie gave her some water, but the exhausted girl had fallen back to sleep immediately. He didn't have to ask what Allie thought of Quincy's condition. Alarm had lines etched on her face, a pinched expression of deep concentration. But there was nothing else to be done—they simply had to hurry.

What were Bryce and Sarah going through with their daughter missing? He had always wanted a child of his own. Maybe he was a cold-blooded killer now, but damned if he'd let something happen to this child.

· · ·

Allison jogged the last hundred yards to the trailhead and blinked back tears. She paused, trying to sense Anton, but her exhausted mind refused to cooperate. If she weren't so tired, she would've been irritated by her powers' illogical, capricious impulses. As it stood, all she wanted was to get in the car.

Peter cradled Quincy, his stubbled jaw clenched as he scanned the area.

He would've been a wonderful father if he'd ever been given the opportunity.

"Think Anton's gone?" she asked. "I can't tell. My radar isn't picking anything up right now."

Peter turned in a slow circle. "I don't think he's here."

They dashed across the trailhead parking area. She opened her car with a spare key she kept hidden under the back bumper, her own set of keys buried under tons of rock. The sedan that had been parked in the lot was long gone, the tire tracks now light indentations in the foot or so of snow on the road. She shuddered at the spots of blood tinting the snow. Anton was still out there somewhere.

Peter turned the heat on high as the car warmed up, and she buckled herself and Quincy into the back seats before turning on her cell phone. As expected, no service.

"I'll call Bryce and Sarah as soon as we get a signal," she said, pillowing Quincy's head in her lap.

He nodded, glancing into the back seat. He drove away, and she willed him to hurry.

As they passed through the town of Joseph, she dialed her sister. "Sarah? We found Quincy." She held the phone away as her sister screamed. "We're taking her straight to the hospital. She'll be okay, but she's pretty dehydrated and has hypothermia."

Sarah mumbled on the other end of the phone, then there was silence and a pause.

Bryce's rough voice sounded like he hadn't slept. "Al?"

"Bryce, hi. Quincy's here. We're in my car, passing through Joseph. Peter's driving. We're making good time."

"I'm going to help." Bryce explained his plan.

"We'll be on the lookout."

"What was that all about?" Peter raised his eyebrow in the rearview mirror.

"Bryce is sending a police escort to bring us into town."

She had one more call to make. "Marcie? It's Doctor Al. Who's on today?"

"Buddy's on. Where are you?"

Allison put force behind her request. "Can I speak with him right this minute?"

There was a pause until her colleague came on the line.

"Buddy, it's Al. I have my niece, Quincy, coming in. She was out in the snow all day yesterday and most of last night. We warmed her up, but she's still out of it and looks dehydrated. An old mine collapsed on us, but I don't think anything's broken."

All business, Buddy asked for basic vitals and observations.

Allison conveyed what she knew, then added, "I haven't mentioned the part about the mine collapse to her parents yet, so if you can hold off on that information for now, that would be great. We'll be there in forty minutes or so."

Turning off the phone, she leaned her head on the seat back. Meeting Peter's reflection in the rearview mirror, she said, "Buddy's a great doctor. He'll have everything ready when we get there."

The fine lines around his eyes crinkled. "I thought you were a great doctor."

"I'm nothing compared to Buddy. He's seen it all." She sighed and relaxed against the seat. Opening one eye, she grinned at Peter. "Well, maybe not everything."

Chapter 20

After dropping off Quincy in the crowd of emergency personnel at the front door of the ER, Allison and Peter walked through the sliding doors. The clank of metal IV poles banging into an instrument stand competed with Buddy's firm, loud orders. The emergency team, like a well-rehearsed orchestra, stabilized Quincy.

Allison leaned against the trauma door and met Buddy's eyes. "Need help?"

He glanced up. "No, we're good here. She's perking up. Go get some rest, Al. You look dead on your feet."

Next to her, Peter stiffened.

"I'd like to wait a while to make sure Quincy's okay," she said.

Buddy called out more orders to nurses and then grinned at Allison. "Then go get cleaned up. You smell funny."

When she took a few steps down the hall, her rubbery legs threatened to give out from under her. All of a sudden, even the effort to stand up became too much.

Peter cupped her elbow. "I'll help."

It had to be exhaustion that weakened her knees. She would *not* feel anything for him, even if he did save Quincy's life, even if the heat of his hand flowed up her arm and into her chest. And she most definitely did not want to know what the rough stubble of his jaw felt like under her lips.

What right did she have to want him close to her? She had rejected him. She had hurt him and then used him. Shame heated her neck. Her heart thudded. He deserved an explanation, and she had no adequate explanation to offer.

Once in the doctor's lounge, he settled in the recliner with a happy groan, picking up the remote. Hilarious. Here was a man born in the early 1900s, but clearly comfortable with the remote control and an easy chair. Maybe some things were timeless ... or genetic.

In her locker she found her spare pair of underwear and a bra. Grabbing a set of scrubs and a towel, she closed the door to the restroom, turned on the hot shower, and stood in the spray as her tired muscles unknotted. It took three washes to get the embedded silt-like dust out of her skin, but finally she felt human again, clean and warm all over.

Relaxed, she exited the restroom in a cloud of steam and then stopped. Peter met her gaze and his eyes darkened. A muscle in his jaw jumped. In the space of time it took to blink, he stood in front of her, only inches away.

She forgot to breathe.

When he shifted his stance, thigh muscles bunched beneath the worn denim jeans, and his blood-stained, torn shirt stretched across his broad chest. The cords in his forearms rolled as his hands fisted and relaxed. He stood silently, watching her.

Her rejection remained an invisible barrier between them.

Time to put on the big girl britches.

She took a deep breath.

"Peter, I owe you an apology."

Swallowing hard, she met his dark brown, speculative gaze and cringed when his brows rose. Disbelief, probably. She couldn't blame him.

Her stomach knotted. "I had no right to judge you. With everything you've been through, your sacrifice for Claire ... "

"You've got to be kidding me."

She flinched at the whip-like lash of his words. "You can't change who you are or what you've been forced to do in the past. If I were faced with a decision like you had with Claire, I would've done the exact same thing."

He said nothing for over a minute. Allison squirmed.

Taking a deep breath, she continued. "And you got hurt up on the mountain because I used you to help get Quincy."

The sharp edge of his voice cut through the still air. "You're apologizing to me?"

Her face burned. "I haven't used anyone like that before, and I am ashamed of my actions. I am truly sorry, Peter."

"Is this a joke?" he said.

Shame descended in a hot cloud. "I shouldn't have acted that way. That's not me, that's not my character. Well, I suppose it is now, but generally I try to accept most folks for who they are. I broke that rule in a big way—"

He sliced his hand through the air, cutting her off. "Don't apologize. Not to me. Not ever. I'm the one that took advantage of you, pushed you too far. And I'm the murderer, remember?" His laugh sounded hollow.

She rocked back on her heels. "I believe I threw myself at you of my own free will."

"I was pretty rough."

"Did it sound like I was complaining?"

Tension radiated from every inch of his tall frame. "What about my criminal behavior?"

She studied his sincere, somber face. "Not to excuse taking someone else's life, but it sounds like you haven't had a choice in the matter over all these years."

"It's still not good."

"Neither is my predicting people dying all over the place."

"But you can't help it."

"Exactly." She peered up into his fathomless eyes and stepped toward him.

He gripped her arms, pushing her out to arm's length. "Allie, I can't—"

Standing on tiptoes, she pulled his head down to kiss him, reveling in the heat from his mouth. His rigid spine relaxed as he leaned toward her. Groaning, he returned the kiss, snaked a rock-hard arm around her waist and pulled her flush to him.

He drew back, jaw muscles clenching spasmodically. "I have nothing to offer. You need something more. I'm barely a man, and one with no future."

"I'm not asking you for any future. Just right now." The truth of those words surprised her. "And my baggage isn't a bargain either."

"You're sure?"

She nodded.

"Anyone use this doctor's lounge much?"

"Only the OB and ER docs."

"Anyone in labor?"

"Nope."

A whoosh of air escaped her as Peter swung her up into his arms.

"Then at least I can do things right this time."

"You didn't—"

He covered her protest with his mouth, holding her securely. Growling, he nipped at her lips. A flame flared deep inside her. Allison wiggled, trying to move into better position to participate, but he held her tightly, his mouth plundering hers. He strolled to the sleep room, shut and locked the door, and settled her on the twin-sized bed as though she were made of the finest china.

When he ran his strong hands through her hair, fanning it over the comforter, his touch on her scalp sent bursts of excitement into her depths. Their connection exploded into full swirling tempest. His desire, his tension, his need—she felt it all in her own mind. She shifted, wanting more, and reached for his shirt. He stilled her hands.

"You first."

He pulled her scrub top up and off. Putting his mouth to her lace bra, he swirled his tongue over her nipple. She gasped at the hot dampness of his mouth on the fabric. He moved to the other side, nibbling through the lace. Cupping her breast, he pinched and rolled her nipple, sending more delicious tingles coursing through her body. At his gentle bite on her breast, she throbbed deep in her groin and moved her hips, trying to relieve the building tension.

He trailed his hand down her abdomen. She shivered, but not from cold, because his hands were just this side of too hot. Her body pulsed for him.

"Roll over," he demanded.

His low voice sent a wave of heat down her spine to her toes. She complied, and he brushed her hair to the side.

Allison froze as he undid her bra clasp and smoothed his hands over her waist, stopping at the band of her scrub pants. Goosebumps rose over her back. The suppressed power of his legs clamped around her hips juxtaposed the gentleness of his fingertips as he created lazy patterns. Relaxed and aroused, she sighed. His amazing lips and teeth would drive her mad, so slowly did he lick his way up and down her spine.

With a low moan, Peter helped her turn over, peeling away the bra. He traced circles over her breasts with the pads of his thumbs as he leaned forward to kiss her deeply. His strong lips nudged her mouth open wide, and he thrust his tongue into her mouth. His mouth demanded, probed, held her in place.

After her head stopped swimming, she returned his passion, tangling her tongue with his. He squeezed her breasts in response, absorbing her quick, excited breaths as she thrashed on the bed beneath him.

Rolling to the side, Peter ran a hand under the waistband of her scrubs inching lower. His hot skin seared her in a path downward.

Allison's hips rose eagerly toward his touch.

He smiled as he cupped her damp curls, teasing her entrance. His eyes were black as midnight.

She locked her gaze onto him as he pulled her scrubs and panties off with one firm tug. When she reached for him, he held her hands away, turning her palms downward on the covers.

"Don't touch me yet. Please." He bit out.

She shuddered when he explored with his lips down her abdomen and lower. She arched toward him, desperate for more.

"Peter, I need—"

"I know."

Intense desire speared through her as he nudged her legs far apart. When he spread the delicate tissue, Allison was completely vulnerable and open. She grasped the bedding as he stroked her. Dampness pooled between her thighs. When he dipped a large finger inside, her muscles clenched.

He held his hand still. Once she relaxed, he slowly curled his finger again, swirls of sensation building up again.

That guttural moan couldn't be hers, could it?

When his obsidian stare met hers, the intensity took her breath away. He removed his hand, grasped her buttocks, and lifted her hips off the bed. With a mischievous smile, he licked his lips and then plunged his mouth into her core.

"Oh!" Hot, liquid waves of passion washed over her. Clutching the covers, she felt strangely suspended as he raised her to his mouth.

When he flicked her nub with his tongue and nipped at her, the muscles of her abdomen involuntarily jumped. He entered her again with two fingers while his mouth roved over her sensitive skin.

Thoughts and emotions and sensations spun together until she couldn't tell where her mind stopped and her body started.

Pressure began to build and she rocked against his mouth, opening her legs farther apart. His groans melded with her sharp gasps until she exploded beneath his lips, shuddering and bowing against the bed. He flicked his tongue over her, and she shuddered again, inner muscles clenching against his fingers.

Keeping his hand inside of her, he lowered her hips back to the bed. With a satisfied gleam that crinkled the lines around his dark eyes, he moved his fingers enough to cause tiny shudders to roll through her.

"Damn your control." Allison let go of the covers, sat up, and ripped his shirt over his head.

Both of them kneeling now, she leaned forward to kiss Peter's muscled chest. Enjoying the scattering of rough hair on his chest, she nuzzled his flat nipples. When she ran her fingernails over the small of his back, he growled low in his throat. She undid the belt clasp, and the snick of his belt exiting the loops broke the silence.

"Allie, be careful," he said, sweat beading his forehead. He actually shook as the muscles on his shoulders bunched tightly. His hands squeezed her waist as she unzipped his jeans.

When she ran her thumb over the glistening, heated tip of his erection, she awakened the sleeping giant.

• • •

Control gone, Peter roared and ripped off his jeans. Flipping her over again, he lifted Allie's hips and pushed her knees forward, relishing the view of her smooth buttocks and lean thighs.

As he parted her folds, the wetness when he caressed her drove him to the edge of sanity. When she quivered and panted as he slipped his fingers in, one and then two, alternating to keep her on edge, he nearly exploded.

At her desperate cries, he knelt behind her hips, his erection teasing her soft entrance. Unable to hold back any longer, he drove into her completely and then held still, a nearly impossible task as he absorbed the mental echoes of her passion.

Connected to Allie and kneeling over her, he ran his hands up and down her back. Leaning forward over her, he pinched one nipple. Her butt jerked in response, sending amazing sensations down his shaft. Peter guided her hips away from him and she whimpered, struggling to slide back onto him. He held her so he teased her further, tormenting them both until she whimpered in frustration.

"I need you now," he breathed.

He brushed her hair forward over one shoulder so he could see her green eyes as she peered at him over the other.

Allison rose up on her forearms, her lean back curved gloriously, rotating her hips in an even sexier curve.

Hell, if he could burn that imagine into his mind, he'd be a happy man for the rest of eternity. Taking several deep breaths to slow things down, he guided her hips over his erection, never quite giving her the entire length. He reached one hand around and caressed her delicate flesh, feeling her silkiness inside and out.

"Peter," she cried, trying to push back against him.

He shifted his knees to spread her legs even further. Pulling her hips up toward him, he plunged into her hard and fast. Peter wanted to brand her as his own. Years of pent-up frustration mixed with the raw desire shared through their connection. He thrust harder, Allie shuddering each time he drove into her. He had to be completely inside her, possess her. She was his. He needed her.

With one hand, he rolled her heated nub, loving how she arched her back and gave a soft moan. *Mine* was his only coherent thought as he pulled her hips back onto his erection. Her muscles spasmed, driving him over the edge. Their cries filled the room as he released into her. Allie fell limp on the blankets, her hips still raised with him inside.

Satisfied by the view of her sweaty, sated body beneath him, he ran his hand down her back and over her curves. When he withdrew from her, the loss of connection created an instant longing to be with her again. Peter turned her over and pulled her into his arms.

Her pupils had become so large, mere slivers of green with tiny glints of gold surrounded them.

"Did I hurt you?"

She shook her head and smiled.

"I shouldn't—"

She cut him off with a kiss and flung her arms around his neck, clinging to him as she shook. He held her tightly, trying to absorb all of her tremors, rubbing her back until she finally calmed down.

When she leaned back, her mossy green gaze was luminous. He'd never seen a woman this beautiful. In wonderment, he ran his fingers over her body, enveloped in his embrace. *Mine*, he thought, as they drifted in the aftermath of their passion.

Chapter 21

One more quick shower later, Allie and Peter left the doctor's lounge. In the ER, they checked on Quincy's status. The girl would stay overnight for observation, but she would recover.

With a nod to the beaming receptionist, Peter exited the ER, Allie by his side, with a whoosh of the sliding doors. He needed to get her home to rest, and he had to formulate a plan to deal with Anton.

They ran directly into Dante and another man.

"Yo, Peter, bro! What the hell happened to you? You look terrible." Dante ran up and pounded him on the arm. His blond hair was fashionably mussed, making him appear like an angel on steroids instead of the massive mess Peter knew him to be.

But he stopped cold when he saw Dante's companion. The balding man was stooped and frail, with liver spots on his forehead and hands, but Peter would've recognized the jaunty glint in those wise eyes anywhere.

"Barnaby?"

"Nice to see you, old friend." He shook Peter's hand. "Now who's old, hmm?"

The happiness his friend exuded spoke volumes of a life well lived. Never mind that it had taken Barnaby four centuries to achieve that—at least he'd done it.

Peter hugged him, careful of the man's hunched back and thin bones.

His friend chuckled. "I might be old, but I won't break. And I'm not blind, either. Hello, my dear!" he said to Allie. He bestowed a courtly kiss to the back of her hand. "You must be the special lady Peter's mentioned. Oh, and did you get a sense of death from me when we shook hands?"

She paled. "I'm not … I didn't … "

In a mock whisper, Barnaby said, "I know you're a Ward, my dear. I'm the one who helped Peter figure it out." He waggled his eyebrows. "Lucky boy, getting you. My Ward was a seventy-year-old Confederate widow. Lovely lady, but her age necessitated more of a platonic relationship, if you know what I mean."

Allie flushed red.

Dante stepped up, plainly appreciating Allie's trim figure in scrubs.

Clearing his throat, Peter stepped in front of her, obscuring Dante's perusal. "So what brings you here, guys? Passing through?" Hopefully his friends would take the hint and not alarm Allie.

But as usual, Dante didn't get any hints unless they were boulder-sized and hurled with great force. "I thought we were helping him kill that guy—" At an arch glare from Barnaby, he clamped his mouth shut.

Allie touched Peter's arm. "Maybe you all want to go somewhere and catch up?"

"It would be nice to talk with my friend, for old time's sake." Barnaby sketched a shallow bow. "Lovely to meet you, milady. I hope to pass time in your pleasant company again in the future." He straightened. "And that sounds possible since you didn't see my death!"

Dante stuck out a massive paw of a hand to Allie. "If he's not good to you"—he motioned toward Peter—"let me know and I'll take care of him. And I'll take care of you, too, if you want." He winked, and Allie blushed again.

Peter extricated her hand from Dante's grip and walked her to the car. "Do you want to stay here at the hospital until we get back?"

She smiled, despite the fatigue etching dark smudges beneath her gold-flecked eyes. "I'll go check on Ivy and run errands in town. There are lots of people around. It'll be fine."

"I don't like it."

She tsked wearily. "It's daylight and business hours. I'll be fine in crowds of shoppers and at the vet office."

"The guys will drop me off at your place." He ran one finger over her soft cheek, loving the spark of connection that arrowed into his groin. "I'll wait for you there. If I'm not there, go back to the hospital."

"I'll be a while in town, so don't worry. And I have a date with my bed, so don't get any fancy ideas. And we still need to talk."

She drove out of the parking lot.

When he turned around, Dante stood right behind him, an appreciative glint in his eyes.

"She's babelicious, bro."

"Dante, enough with the slang. You're 300 years old."

Dante flashed a superstar-white smile. "Keeps me young, my friend."

Barnaby shuffled over. "Let's go someplace to talk, gentlemen."

"Well, one of you needs to drive. My transportation left," Peter said.

"Shotgun!" Dante called out.

"You idiot, you're the driver," Peter groaned as they approached the Hummer.

"You know any place good to eat?" Barnaby asked. "I'm rather peckish."

"There are some places near the interstate where we can get a cup of coffee."

"Or lunch?" Dante asked.

Damn Dante and his bottomless stomach. It would have to be Denny's. Once they were seated, his friend proceeded to order three entrées, rubbing his belly in anticipation. Dante hadn't gotten the memo about the Indebted not having much of an appetite.

Barnaby dipped his head and chuckled. "What about your fetchingly girlish figure?"

Dante grinned broadly. "Doesn't change, no matter how much or how little I eat. So I might as well enjoy!" He studied the waitress's cleavage when she leaned over to place their drinks on the table.

"What exactly are you enjoying, Dante?" Peter asked.

His friend unwrapped his silverware, the fork and knife disappearing in his big hands. "Everything, bro! Opportunities are all around, gastronomical and carnal. The world is my *smorgåsbord*."

Once the food arrived, Peter couldn't wait any longer to get to the point. "So why're you two here anyway?"

"Helping you out, my boy. Jerahmeel sent you a rank bastard. I heard a little about what happened to that child and your lady. They could've died."

"How'd you know that?"

"Police scanner in Dante's car. Comes in handy." The lines in the old man's face deepened as he grinned.

Peter gripped the coffee mug. Yeah, given Quincy's limp body and Allie gasping for breath as the mine collapsed behind them, it was a miracle they hadn't died.

Dante pointed to the cracks in Peter's ceramic mug. "Whoa, bro, ease up there. Don't go making a mess."

"Sorry." With effort, he relaxed his hand. "You were saying, Barnaby?"

"This minion, he's the worst I've spied. And after 400-some years, I've seen some bad people in this line of business."

Peter rubbed his temple. "I wounded him pretty badly."

"Doesn't matter. Might slow him down for a few days or a few weeks."

"What if I leave town and never return?" He'd do it in a heartbeat if it kept Allie and her family safe.

"You don't understand, my boy. Of course if you complete your contract, that's bad for Jerahmeel's power supply. The problem is, if you're not working for them, then they want to make what life you have remaining a living hell. You know that they'll try to take away all that you love so you suffer torment until you finally die of natural causes. The rules bind me from telling you specific details, but please know that I feared gravely for Jane's life."

"What are you saying?" Cold dread speared Peter's gut.

"Anyone connected to you is not safe. Doesn't matter if you're here or on the other side of the world, they know. And that's how they're going to get to you."

"So I have to find the minion and kill him."

Barnaby and Dante nodded.

"And keep anyone I care about, and everyone *she* cares about, safe?"

They nodded again.

Peter laughed. "What about Jerahmeel simply coming in behind the minion and finishing the job himself? He's powerful enough to do it."

Barnaby rubbed his sagging jowls. "He cannot involve himself directly. Also, my boy, recognize that the Meaningful Kill is not so much about the numbers of kills or the types of kills, but about you."

"I don't understand."

"I know, and I can't give you more information. You'll figure it out. But what I can tell you is that Jerahmeel is not allowed to physically impact what happens here on Earth. That's why we must provide him with nourishment, when we take the life forces into the knives. That's why he created minions to destroy people."

"What do you mean, 'figure it out'? It's not Anton I have to kill?"

"Maybe not. I've said too much, my boy, but you're close."

Peter blew out a long breath. "So all I need to do is keep anyone near me safe, destroy the minion before he kills everyone, and somehow figure out the Meaningful Kill on my own."

Barnaby nodded.

Dante continued to pillage his five-course meal.

"Sounds easy enough," Peter quipped. "Which part are you two helping me with?"

Dante paused after consuming most of a baked potato in one bite. His grin would have been handsome if it weren't for the malicious glint in his baby blue, killing-machine eyes. "Any part you'd like. I'll give you dibs on killing the minion yourself, even though we all know I'd do a better job. He did attack the woman you love and an innocent girl."

Peter sputtered. "I never said I loved her."

"Verily, it's written all over your face," Barnaby said. "Don't fight it. It's a beautiful thing, love. They write sonnets about such things."

"Love sure is a beautiful thing," Dante added.

"Since when have you loved anyone but yourself?"

"Just the other day, I loved two women. Over and over and over." Dante crammed a forkful of steak, pancake, and French fries into his mouth.

"No, you moron. Love, love. Not sex."

Sadness passed over Dante's easygoing countenance as he chewed and swallowed. "Long time ago, bro. But you know how it goes. Can't get attached to anyone in this line of work. You outlive 'em, and that's a real bummer."

"Okay, fair enough. So how're we going to flush out this guy—" Peter bent over double.

He couldn't breathe.

It felt like his ribs had been crushed.

"What is it?" Barnaby asked.

No air.

His head throbbed. Waves of terror flooded his senses, threatening to overload him. Allie. Her gift. Their connection. He could feel her.

Hell.

The minion had found her.

. . .

Allison studied her house for five full minutes. Nothing out of place. No movement. Peter should be here any minute. Good enough. All she wanted was to crawl under the covers of her bed.

She turned off her car and clicked the garage door closed. After surviving the panicked activity of the last twenty-four hours, the silence of her house settled into her bones with a torpid weight. With immense effort, she trudged into the kitchen, setting grocery bags on the countertop, the crinkle of paper loud in the silent house. She missed Ivy's greeting, but at least her dog was improving.

Fatigue made Allison's eyes scratchy, and she yawned as she kicked off her shoes. Dimly, she reminded herself to put a spare change of clothes in her locker at work.

Mid-yawn, she froze and stared at the kitchen faucet. It had never dripped before. But they'd left in such a hurry to track down Quincy yesterday, it might not have been turned off properly.

Walking over to the sink, she almost stepped on a shiny spot on the kitchen floor. As she knelt down, she caught the scent of metal—the tang of blood.

Blood.

Oh God.

Heart pounding, she tiptoed back around the counter.

Don't make a sound.

She listened hard. Nothing.

But she sensed it—a pressure change in the atmosphere.

A familiar tingling started in her fingertips. She closed her hand around the key and backed toward the door to the garage.

Fingers and head buzzing, she turned the doorknob.

The door exploded inward, knocking her backward onto the floor. A seething, bloody Anton lunged at her. "Hello, delicious lady."

Adrenaline coursing, she scrambled to her feet, pivoted, and ran toward the front door. He reached her before she opened it, yanked her back by the hair, and threw her to the ground.

Stars burst in front of her eyes as the world spun around her.

He stood over her with a barking laugh. "Oh my, we're going to have such special fun together."

She tore her fingernails on the wood floor, trying to crawl away, until he ground a booted foot into her thigh and pinned her to the floor. Her thigh muscle knotted under his weight.

"Tsk, tsk, bad manners." His eye twitched and he tapped at his temple. "First of all, you shouldn't sit around when a guest walks in. You should get right up and offer him a drink."

When she didn't respond, Anton stepped off of her leg. He reached down and grabbed the front of her scrub top, yanking her up to stand before him. His dark eyes bulged. "Well?"

He was in some sick fantasy. What could she do? When would Peter be here? Maybe she could play along and buy some time.

"May I offer you something to drink?" she choked out.

Abruptly, his demeanor shifted to one of insane politeness. "Why, yes, madam, I would like a glass of your best wine, if you please." He released her, chuckling when she stumbled.

She limped into the kitchen.

Anton trailed after her, muttering and tapping his forehead.

Wet blood soaked the front of his shirt. Dark red smudges of dried blood coated the top of his head where he periodically scratched at the skin.

How injured was he? Could she slow him down? She retrieved a wine glass and bottle with shaking hands. After four tries with the corkscrew, she popped it loose and poured him a glass of red wine. As he accepted the beverage, she backed along the counter, sidling toward her cutlery set.

He turned to set the glass down.

She jammed a knife into his arm.

Howling in rage, he ripped the knife out and hurled her sideways into the opposite wall. At a sickening snap, blinding pain flooded her neck and shoulder. She couldn't breathe. After a wave of nausea plowed over her, she tried to identify the injury. When she moved her shoulder, the collarbone ground together with the sound of chalk scraping on a blackboard.

Anton slapped her with a slick, bloody hand, whipping her head to the side.

Was the blood she tasted hers?

He pinned her to the wall.

Allison's useless left arm dangled at her side.

"Oh, you've injured yourself, my dear."

She screamed when he pressed against her damaged collarbone and would have crumpled if he hadn't held her upright.

"You poor thing, no one here to protect you from little old me."

Anton propped her up against the kitchen wall, using pressure on her shifting collarbone to get her attention. She almost passed out from the pain.

"Why are you doing this?" she wheezed. She attempted to collect enough mental focus to call to Peter, but her overloaded mind couldn't do it.

A muscle twitched in his right eyelid. "Because of your lover, that's why."

"I don't understand."

"He's on the verge of completing his contract." He made a *tsking* sound and wagged his finger, staring at the tip of his finger in fascination. After a moment, he blinked and refocused on her. "We all know that ending a contract with the big boss is a big no-no. Nobody gets out of a contract." He paused. "Well, almost no one."

Barnaby.

She took a careful breath. "What does this have to do with me?"

"Ah, yes, you, you, you. Me, me, me. I wanna talk about me."

He began singing a country song by the same title. Reason wouldn't work, so she hummed the song along with him until he ran out of steam.

He snapped his bloodshot gaze back to her. "Now where were we?"

She cringed away from his breath, foul like a sunbaked corpse. He had a few missing teeth where only bloody pulps remained.

"Ah yes. You, you, you … "

While he sang, she tried to collect herself enough to call to Peter. She closed her eyes and got a burst out right before Anton leaned into her shoulder again. The two pieces of her collarbone ground together. She screamed, the blackness closing in.

He grabbed her chin. "Pay attention, lovely, lovely. It's rude to think about other things when I'm talking. So if your boyfriend figures out his Meaningful Kill, he'll be done with the contract. The big boss hates that. Hates it, hates it, hates it. Once an employee, always an employee. So he wants to make Peter pay." Giggling, he sang, "Peter pay, Peter pay, bossy'll make Peter pay."

When he let up the pressure for a moment, Allison sucked air into her lungs, formulating her next move against this nut job. Nothing obvious came to mind.

He said, "So you're the piece of torture, see?"

"No, I don't see," she cried.

"Even if Peter finishes the contract, he'll have nothing to live for anymore. I'm going to destroy anyone he cares about. You. That delightful little girl. Her parents. Maybe his friend Barnaby if I can track him down."

Her heart plunged into an airless vacuum. "No. You can't kill my family. They haven't done anything wrong." A tear ran unchecked down her cheek as terror and pain mixed. She had to stop him.

"Sorry, rules are rules," he said, tapping his forehead rhythmically. "But maybe we can make a deal. You do some nice things for me." He licked his chapped lips with his bloody tongue. "And I'll make your family members' deaths swift. If you're not nicey-nicey to me, well, then … it could take a while."

"You're an animal."

Panic overwhelmed her as she kicked at him. He merely pressed his hand against her collarbone, stilling her with the cruel pressure.

"*Rowr.*" He growled and made a claw.

He stopped mid-paw and stared at his hand for what seemed like an eternity. His bloodshot eyes brightened, and he focused intently on Allison with a toothless smile.

"I have an idea that's going to get me in good with the big boss. Okay, you just stand there against the wall." He reached down to his leg and pulled out a knife similar to Peter's. "So while I'm in the process of torturing you to death, I can also get loads of your life force for the big guy to dine on tonight. He might promote me. No one's ever supped on a Ward's spirit. Yummy."

He pointed the tip of the knife at Allison's sternum and pressed hard enough to draw blood.

She screamed as the blade seared her like a hot poker.

Anton drew the knife downward, slicing her scrub top in two. "Take that shirt off, lovely, lovely. I want a pristine canvas to work with."

She eased her right arm out of the top, and then used it to slide the shirt off her useless left arm. In a bra and scrub pants, she leaned against the wall, her knees threatening to buckle.

"Now, how well you stand there and let me play will determine how nice I am to your family when I kill them."

The knife glowed with a greenish hue when he traced it over her sternum. As he slid it up and brought it flat against her face, the blade heated and hummed next to her ear.

Oh God, what a way to die. If she could hold still through the hurt, maybe she could help her family.

Sweat beaded his forehead. Stale steam rose from the pores of his skin.

"Oh my, my, my. The hard part will be going slowly with you. Don't want to waste any of your blood, yummy scrummy, yummy scrummy."

Allison froze in horror, fixated on the blade now glowing bright green and poised over her skin.

He drew the knife down her arm, the blood blooming red. She burned beneath the razor-sharp blade. Turning to her torso, he trailed the knife in an agony of art along her ribcage.

She couldn't hold in the screams as Anton held her in place by her shattered collarbone and continued his slow work, laughing as her blood ran onto the floor.

• • •

Dante braked violently at the entrance to Allie's dirt lane. Peter jumped out and sprinted toward the house with Dante at his heels.

Her screams were audible even outside the house, and her terror banged inside Peter's head. Caring about nothing but getting to her, he dove through the dining room window and rolled on the shattered glass. Allie, her upper body naked save for a blood-soaked bra, stood upright by virtue of Anton's grip on her shoulder.

Peter stopped in his tracks. Lurid lines crisscrossed her arms and chest and abdomen. Blood flowed and pooled on the floor. Her glassy eyes were unfocused.

Was she even alive?

Dante crunched broken glass as he stepped up behind him. "*Herre Gud!*" his friend swore in his native tongue.

Anton smiled and dragged the flat of the blade over her cheek.

Peter lost the edges of his vision as his entire world narrowed down to a bloody Allie sagging under Anton's hand.

"You like my work? I'm quite the artist. See?" He waved the glistening, glowing blade. Anton's giggle raked across Peter's nerves. "It likes this one. Delicious."

"You bastard!" He launched himself at the minion.

He didn't reach her in time.

Anton plunged the knife into her lower chest.

The tiny, pitiful sound that escaped her pale lips set off an explosion in Peter's mind.

He hurled Anton away, crashing the minion into the kitchen table.

Her right hand shaking, Allie pulled the glowing knife out of her chest and slid down the wall, blood squirting from the wound.

Torn, Peter looked from her broken body to Anton, who was sprawled on the floor on his hands and knees, trying to rise.

"Dante?"

"Oh, yeah. I'll take care of this one, Petey."

His friend stalked toward Anton, his giant legs pounding the floor. Dante's ice-blue eyes had turned cold and black.

"This *oåkting* will pay." Dante planted one foot and viciously kicked Anton in the head, leveling the minion to the ground.

The minion tried to crawl away, but with one thunderous stomp to Anton's midsection, Dante broke the minion's spine in a sickening crack, temporarily paralyzing him. He didn't wait for the minion to heal. Anton's pleas fell on deaf ears as Dante drew his knife and ran the minion through slowly and repeatedly. He then hacked Anton's head from his body and let it drop to the floor with a *thunk*.

Peter fell to his knees in the pool of Allie's sticky blood, pulling her against him. She breathed rapidly, gurgling. Air whooshed in and out of her chest wound. He put his hand on the wound to close it.

"Dante! Get me ointment and a cloth. Hurry."

Dante blinked until his black eyes became blue again and ran off in search of supplies.

"Allie," Peter whispered. Real tears rolled down his face, the first time since 1945.

He felt the buzz of their mental connection growing weaker. She was drifting away from him, like a boat floating from shore.

Her green eyes flickered open. Little blood vessels had burst in the whites. She licked her swollen lower lip. Her wet cough drove a wave of nausea through Peter.

Allie weakly lifted her right hand to touch his chest. "You're okay," she said. "Quincy? Sarah?"

"They're fine, Allie. They're safe."

"No, he's going to kill them, too." When she closed her eyes, a teardrop rolled out of one corner.

"He's dead now. He can't hurt them." Peter caressed her cheek. "I'm so sorry for everything. I'm sorry I brought this down on you."

She inhaled rapidly as she shook her head. "My choice," she gasped out. "Thank you … "

Her bloodied body. This torture. Her fear. Every bit of it was his fault. It had to stop. He had to stop. The answer clicked as Barnaby entered the house. Peter's world was over without her.

"Good Lord, son, is she alive?" The older man put a hand out to her bruised neck.

"Barely. Please call an ambulance."

"Dante can get there faster," Barnaby said.

"I know, but she needs oxygen right away. The ambulance is safer."

Barnaby picked up the phone and gave dispatch the information.

Dante returned with a tube of Neosporin and strips of bed sheets. Even the unshakable Swede paled and turned away at the sight of Allie's injuries.

Peter squirted ointment on the fabric and pressed it over the sucking chest wound to create a seal, willing her to stay alive.

Dante reappeared with a sheet and gently draped it over Allie. He shook his head. "The minion's death was much too swift. I wish I could kill him again for this, bro."

"Me too, Dante."

They met the EMTs in the driveway, where Peter laid an unconscious Allie on the gurney. The ambulance personnel placed an oxygen mask on her while electrodes recorded her rapid heartbeat. The medics transferred her to the ambulance and sped off, lights blazing and sirens blaring.

The house was deathly silent. Blood covered the kitchen walls and floor. Peter stared in shock at his soaked clothes. He hadn't said goodbye to her. He might never get the chance.

"We'll clean up before the police get here," Dante said.

Barnaby nodded. "Go wash up. You'll want to stay with your lady. They won't let you in the hospital if you're covered in blood. And when you're done at the hospital, you come get me. We'll talk about what needs to be done."

Peter stopped dead in his tracks. The Meaningful Kill. He understood.

Barnaby smiled sadly.

Chapter 22

Allison's life boiled down to brief flashes of images.

There was a prick on her arm in the bouncing vehicle as an EMT placed an IV. She tried to answer his questions, but blackness covered her again in a blissful blanket.

Bright lights shone overhead. Buddy stood over her, his kind face creased with worry as he called out rapid-fire orders.

Odd, he's normally quite calm.

She heard her own desperate rasping. She clawed at her throat. Couldn't get enough air. Gentle hands held her arms down. She heard the air poofing in and out of her sucking chest wound.

An open pneumothorax sounds different when I'm the patient.

Buddy's mumbled apology as he prepped for a chest tube placement. The fire of thousands of intercostal nerves flaring when Buddy drove the tube between her ribs and up and into her pleural space.

A tidal wave of darkness.

Sarah's tears, her cool hands touching Allison's bruised cheek.

Buddy's call for four units of O negative blood, run wide open.

Allison knew why he was asking for that much blood. *Well, that's bad.*

A rumbling movement as the OR crew and anesthesiologist ran her gurney down the hall. Fluorescent lights flashed above her bed.

One, two, blank. One, two, blank.

A bump as they entered the OR.

The general surgeon, his gruff face hidden by a mask, bent over to talk with her about bleeding thoracic vessels. Her lung remained collapsed despite the chest tube. He needed to fix both issues.

Yup, that sounds about right.

Also he mentioned that the orthopedic surgeon would be in to repair her collarbone.

Roger. Whatever they have to do.

She skimmed along in rolling waves of agony until the anesthesiologist covered her nose and mouth with a bag valve mask and cranked up what she hoped was isoflurane. She slid into a painless abyss.

No air, but blackness. Allison was back in the mine. Her chest ached. Throat sore, she wanted to rub her neck, but her arms wouldn't move. Struggling, she realized her left arm was fixed in place across her body. And she was intubated, which felt like drowning alive as the machine regulated her breathing.

Stay calm, ride the vent.

Easier said than done. She needed to remember how this felt when she intubated patients in the ER in the future.

Maybe the nurses would turn up the Propofol drip so she could go back to sleep. Allison couldn't speak. The tube and beeps and pain were starting to get to her.

I can't exactly ask for help.

Quiet beeps punctuated the ventilator sounds.

In, *whoosh*, out, *click*. In, *whoosh*, out, *click*.

Warmth started in her right hand and traveled through her chest out to her head and toes. Her entire body relaxed.

She was pain-free.

That makes no sense.

She curled her hand into the heated hand that held hers, and she met Peter's dark brown gaze. She wanted to touch his rough cheek, but couldn't work up the energy.

"Allie." His voice cracked.

She started to get mental feedback from his anguish and tried to block him but couldn't un-fuzz her brain enough to do so.

Pain, not physical but mental, pressed down on her mind. All she wanted to do was reassure Peter that she would be okay.

That he would be okay.

Why wouldn't he be okay?

So she rode the vent and the waves of pain coming from Peter. She pushed against his agony with her love for him.

Love?

Oh God, no. She had no intention of falling in love with him. The plan was to find a normal man, right?

He lifted his head. "You're crying. Are you in pain?"

That's not why I'm crying.

"I'll get the nurse," he said.

His warmth was gone, but his pain continued to flow into her mind, relentless waves of torture. Something sliced into her chest. Or was it his chest?

He called to her, as if from a great distance. As if he were being pulled away.

Away.

She searched along the faded lines of pain.

Silence. Had she imagined him?

"Al?"

Allison squinted against the fluorescent lights.

Sarah's haggard face was wet, her eyes red-rimmed. "You're awake."

When Allison tried to reply, the tube abraded her throat.

Don't fight the vent.

Sarah was gone, replaced by an ICU nurse.

"Want off the vent?" The nurse studied the flow sheet.

Allison nodded carefully, the endotracheal tube scraping with the movement.

"Okay, Dr. Al, you know the drill." The nurse deflated the ET tube balloon. "Give me a few good coughs."

Allison complied despite searing agony in her ribs. By her third or fourth cough, the tube was out. The nurse placed a Venturi mask with its stale, plastic, oxygen scent over Allison's mouth and nose. She welcomed the oxygen over face.

Sarah's face floated back into view. "How's your pain?"

"Decent," Allison whispered. "The worst is my right side."

"Not surprising. Dr. Bart had to open your chest to stop the bleeding. And you still have a chest tube. You'll be sore for a while."

"Quincy?"

"She's receiving IV fluids. She had some frostbite on one foot and might have a little nerve damage but should be fine. She's demanding ice cream now. I left Bryce to sit with her for a while. She's driving me nuts. But you and Peter did a good thing finding my girl." Tears rolled down Sarah's cheeks as she leaned into Allison's one-armed embrace.

"It was Peter who saved Quincy."

"No, it was a joint effort. You two make quite the team."

Allison's smile cracked a swollen lip. "I know. That's the problem."

"What's the problem? You like him and he likes you."

"It's not that simple with me, and you know it. I want a normal relationship with a normal man."

"I know you do, sis. You've always wanted that."

"I can't have that with Peter."

Sarah patted Allison on the leg. "You of all people should understand. In life you sometimes get what you need, not what you want."

"Speaking of Peter, where is he?"

Sarah didn't meet her eyes. "We haven't seen him since last night."

• • •

"What are we doing?" Dante asked from the driveway of Allie's house.

Peter rubbed his chin. "You can't come with me. But if you can stick around La Grande for a while and watch over Allie, I'd appreciate it." The image her of last night, laying on the hospital bed with all the wires and electrodes attached to her, haunted him.

"Anything, bro. When are you returning?"

Peter glanced at Barnaby, who shrugged.

"No idea," Peter said. "Not even sure I'll return."

Dante's eyebrows rose.

"But I have to try."

"Well, then good luck to you. I'll watch over your lady." Uncharacteristically serious, he clapped Peter on the arm and took off for the hospital.

Peter turned to the stooped old man. "All right, now what?"

"I don't know. There's no manual for this kind of thing."

"How'd you do it?"

"You know I can't give details." He rubbed his bald head. "But I might suggest you go somewhere private and safe, where you have some connection to humanity. Where you find meaning. Where you can focus."

Peter squinted at the sunny sky. "Can you still hike?"

"Not quickly, but yes."

"I can give you the Sherpa treatment up there. I don't know about coming back down."

"I'll manage, son."

They stopped in the local outdoor store and picked up warm clothes for Barnaby, sleeping bags, backpacks, and food. Throwing everything in the back of the truck, Peter drove back up to Wallowa Lake. Both men rode in pensive silence, broken only by the slush hitting the wheel wells of the truck.

"Will it work? Getting out of my contract?" Peter finally spoke.

"If it does, you'll be the second person in the last century, that I know of, who has tried it and succeeded."

"But you can't tell me anything about how to do this?"

"No. You have to do what you feel is right. You already have an idea of how to proceed. I've seen it on your face." Creases bracketed Barnaby's wise eyes. "I'll be there to help minister to you in any way needed."

"Sounds like it could be bad."

"I wish I'd had someone there to help me when I completed my contract."

Peter nodded in appreciation. "Anyone who hasn't succeeded?"

"Verily, I think I'm the only other person who's thought to try." He chuckled, stretching gnarled fingers until they popped. "I had an excellent reason, too. My Jane was the most lovely woman." He smiled sadly. "Maybe anyone who succeeded years ago simply got old and died of natural causes?"

"That sounds nice right about now."

"I know precisely what you mean."

They pulled into the trailhead parking lot, right where Allie and Peter had started their search for Quincy. Their old tracks were still visible, although the snow had melted some with the warmer weather today. Shouldering the heavy backpack, Peter started hiking. When the trail became steeper, he offered to give Barnaby a lift.

The older man shook his head. "So far so good. I might be old, but I'm not completely decrepit. Not bad for over 400 years old, hmm?" He took a deep breath and blew it out. "But let's keep the pace nice and slow."

"Sure thing."

When they reached the cabins near Aneroid Lake, Barnaby whistled. "This place is beautiful."

"I didn't stop to sightsee last time I was here, but you're right, it's nice."

Peter led them to the hiking club yurt and opened the door. In unspoken agreement, he set the fire and they settled down for the night on the two remaining pallets.

He had no idea what to expect tomorrow. No set plan. All he wanted was to free Allie from the evil that dogged him, and to do that, Peter would have to separate himself from the evil.

Would he survive?

Was that even the point?

Allie had made it clear she wanted a relationship with a normal man. If he became human again, would that be enough for her? After the decades of evil deeds, would she accept someone like him?

Who cared?

Bottom line was Allie's safety. As long as she was out of danger, he'd live out his years as a hermit but have satisfaction knowing she'd be safe.

If anything else came out of his actions tomorrow, well that would be a bonus.

• • •

The next morning, he woke with a belly full of churning hope and dread. He'd finalized his plan late last night. It seemed logical. Besides, there were no other options. God, he hoped his hunch was correct. If he was wrong? Well, at minimum, Allie would be safe.

The day began cold and clear, with ice covering Aneroid Lake and the granite cirque that shadowed it on one side. Pine trees dotted the terrain, and birds chirped in the spring sunshine.

He should've enjoyed the scenery, but he had work to do. Barnaby couldn't give him any pointers, so Peter operated on instinct. Going down to the lake, he used an axe to chop ice away from the shore, opening up a ten-foot section. The clear water lapped on the snowy shore.

Hauling supplies from the yurt, Peter spread out a large tarp and placed several items on it.

The lines on Barnaby's face deepened.

After completing the preparations he felt were necessary, Peter motioned for Barnaby to approach.

"Barnaby, could you stand over there but be available just in case? I don't know how I'll be afterward."

"I'll be right here, son," his old friend said.

Peter shed his clothing as he stood on the tarp near the shore. When this was all over, he'd either be alive or dead. There would be absolutely nothing in between.

Completely naked, he was oblivious to the crisp air in his non-human state. To begin, he recounted as many of his kills as he could remember. The faces, the screams, the hot smell of fear. He forced himself to recall Claire in the iron lung and the choice he made to go down this path. Even knowing what he did now, he'd sell his soul again to save her life. And then he thought about Allie's bloody and broken body on the gurney.

He unsheathed the blade on his leg, its green glow apparent even in the bright sunlight. His hand shook. He knew what the Kill meant to him. Hopefully, he wasn't overthinking a trick question here, but the answer felt right. And Barnaby had told him to follow his instincts.

Peter focused all of his energy on Allie's sweet face. She brought light to his darkness. Even her unnecessary apology gave him hope that there might be a future for someone like him.

She showed him that his life wasn't worthless.

His life was worth her life.

He gritted his teeth and stared up at the blue sky.

And plunged the knife under his ribcage.

Fighting the instinct to withdraw, he took one last breath and shoved the blade upward, piercing his heart. Fire exploded through his torso.

Peter crashed to the tarp as his life's blood flowed into the lake. Molten torture coursed through his limbs, followed by ice-cold lassitude. The glowing green blade lodged in his chest pulsed hungrily as it consumed his life force.

Just as he started to lose consciousness, a loud rumble startled him. The ground shook. A scent of pungent rotten eggs permeated the air.

Jerahmeel's sinister and immaculately dressed form blocked out the morning sun as his palpable anger washed over Peter. Jerahmeel loomed over him. "Disgusting. What a disappointment."

His voice bounced off the granite mountainside and vibrated through the frozen ground into Peter's skull. "You're worthless to me now. I do so wish I could kill you myself. But rules are rules. If you should survive, let me torment you further with the thought of my return. Cherish the rest of your pathetic existence. Whatever you do, never, ever attract my attention. If I become interested in you again, I will find you. And anyone you care for. Anywhere."

"Yes, my lord Jerahmeel," Peter managed to choke out. This was the last time he would have to use that phrase.

The demon scowled at Barnaby as Peter sprawled on the tarp. With Peter's life blood gushing out, he was helpless to protect Barnaby.

Jerahmeel seethed. "Did you tell him to do this? You know I don't abide interference." He patted his perfect curls. "I could destroy you with my bare hands."

"No, sire, I didn't tell him anything. And, yes, I know you have the power to destroy me, but if I understand the rules, you cannot, *my lord*."

Jerahmeel roared into the cold air; his evil echoes loosened rocks that crashed from the top of the cirque into the valley below. The ground beneath Peter shuddered and heaved, like it would swallow him whole.

Barnaby said, "You're older than even I, Jerahmeel, but I've learned a few things over all these years."

"Silence, old man."

"What are you going to do, condemn me to an eternal hell on Earth? You already did that. I escaped it." Barnaby wheezed in the cold air. "You must leave this boy alone, per the rules to which you are committed."

"Fine. But if he survives, make sure he keeps his mouth shut. May you both die soon and with great suffering." He pinned Peter with a nasty stare.

Peter nodded weakly.

"And that Ward? Your *amour*? Did she survive?"

You can't have her, you bastard.

"I don't know," Peter whispered.

"She reminds me of someone I know. Someone delectable. Ah, yes, now I know. Someone I'd like to have for myself ... Perhaps later." He licked his ruby-red lips, bizarre eyes avid. "Too bad you forfeited your chance to know."

"Stay away from Allie," Peter rasped.

Jerahmeel shook his head. "If you survive, you'd best make sure that Ward keeps her skills to herself." He paused, snow melting around his shiny leather shoes. "Personally, I'd prefer for you to simply fail."

Peter blinked into the bright sky as Jerahmeel leaned over. Cloying sulfurous smoke clogged Peter's nostrils. He was having trouble keeping his eyes open but fought for every last bit of air to stay conscious.

Keep Allie safe.

Jerahmeel reached down, then twisted and ripped the glowing knife out of Peter's torso, sneering as Peter jerked in agony. "I hope this hurts like hell and you perish, regardless of your so-called noble efforts. You are a worthless, *pathétique* human."

Torrents of blood gushed out as Peter's life ebbed away.

Jerahmeel gave the men one last contemptuous glare, and with another tremor of the earth, he disappeared.

Peter's vision dimmed as Barnaby knelt next to him. He wanted to focus only on Allie and her sweet face. He felt her echo. One last flicker of contact, a guttering flame. If she survived, then maybe he had succeeded after all?

The last pint of blood drained out of his body. Jerahmeel hadn't killed him, he had simply removed the knife. Peter's laser-accurate strike had taken care of the Kill. His mind went blank as he took a final breath.

Peter's undead heart stopped.

• • •

No birds chirped. A slight breeze disturbed the small area of exposed water. Little sloshes of water upon smooth pebbles broke the silence in the chilly, clear air. Barnaby contemplated his deceased friend and glanced around once more for Jerahmeel.

"Peter, my boy, I hope you've figured out Rule Number One. The one thing that breaks the contract." Barnaby spoke to the pale body of his friend on the tarp.

Had Peter done it? Only time would tell.

He had no recollection of how long his own body had lain on the ground, soaking the soil with his blood. He simply counted himself lucky to have awakened as a human.

What should he do now? The idea of washing oneself clean and being reborn seemed like a good plan. With gnarled, arthritic hands, he rolled Peter's bloody body into the frigid lake. His friend slipped beneath the surface. With a resigned sigh, Barnaby sat on the clean portion of tarp and waited.

Chapter 23

It had been more than two weeks since she and Peter had found Quincy at Aneroid Lake. Back home now, Allison and Ivy were up to walking for ten minutes at a time, very slowly.

She smiled at her limping dog, whose tail still wagged. Ivy flashed a happy doggy grin. Ivy hadn't left Allison's side since they'd been reunited on the way home from Grande Ronde Hospital. Allison had a hard time corralling the giant canine's exuberance, for both their sakes.

Walking on flat ground, careful not to jar her right chest or her left shoulder, Allison gingerly inhaled the cool spring air. Against the clear blue skies, the snow-covered Wallowa Mountains rose to the east. Today, the sun shone brightly today on the fields, bright green with spring growth. She should've been grateful to be alive, but her soul was as empty as a home where all the occupants had fled.

While she was in the hospital, Allison had experienced shocking feedback from her connection with Peter. She had pressed back into the connection with her love for him, and tried to push her love through that link.

Then nothing.

Their low-level connection had ceased. The void hurt more than the aches from her wounds. Allison had cast her mind about over the past days, trying to get a sense of Peter, but all that remained was a lonely vacuum.

Whatever he had done, he had suffered. Without any sense of him whatsoever, she knew in her heart that he was dead.

She now understood *takotsubo* cardiomyopathy, "broken heart syndrome." Her lungs burned when she breathed, her head pounded like a hammer on an anvil, and her heart ached like it couldn't expand properly. There would never be another man like Peter in her life, but he had left her behind to carry on her mundane human existence. Alone.

She tried to put on a brave face for folks at the hospital and for her family, but upon arriving home she politely asked everyone to give her some space. With piles of well-intended casseroles stocked in the fridge, she faced her loss in miserable solitude.

Reaching the end of the lane, Allison winced as Ivy's tug on the leash jarred her collarbone. Anton's pressure had displaced it and torn surrounding tissue. The orthopedic surgeon had plated her collarbone at the same time as her thoracotomy. The fracture site ached, but she knew it would knit more quickly now.

A black Hummer approached with the window rolled down. Angry gangster rap poured out of the vehicle. Ever cheerful, Dante poked his blond head out.

"Doing okay?"

"Fine, thanks for checking," she said.

He smiled. "Need anything?"

She shook her head and turned slowly around as Dante drove off.

He'd checked on her daily since Peter left, and she was certain it was on Peter's orders that he did so. Poor guy. She bet he'd rather be anywhere but here, babysitting an invalid.

The one time Dante had touched her skin, she got a small buzz of connection. He was, after all, death, and detecting death was, after all, her specialty.

She smiled to herself. All the nice people had offered up help and condolences, shook her hand, and hugged her. In the past she would've had a bad vision by now. Her "gift" resurfaced at times, but at least she could block it more easily now, much to her relief. Hopefully in the future she could learn to open herself up again.

And Quincy was alive, representing the first time a vision had led Allison to *prevent* a death. She had a pretty powerful skill, and now she wanted to try to use it. Maybe she could help save someone else in the future. Maybe.

Faintly, she heard a vehicle door slam behind her on the road. Expecting to see Dante coming back with another question, she nearly kept walking. Thinking better of it, she turned to see Peter's truck idling at the end of the dirt road, with Barnaby at the wheel. The old man bowed his bald head with a flourish of his hand and then pulled away.

Peter stood in the middle of the road.

Blood drained to Allison's feet as she stared in disbelief.

He approached her, haltingly, as though each step took a massive effort.

Lightheaded, she stood still, blinking to make sure she wasn't imaging things. Ivy yipped, and then sat, as if sensing the gravity of the situation.

Peter stopped, inches away. Was he a ghost?

Dropping the leash, Allison placed a shaking hand on his very corporeal chest. His heart beat steadily beneath her fingertips.

She moved her hand to her own heart and leaned forward with a choked cry. Their mental link clicked into place as he guided her into his chest, connecting them physically, too. The comfortable blanket of their link settled on her so softly.

Sobs racked her body as she wept into him her fear and anger. She fisted the fabric of his shirt and held on tightly. If she let go, she feared he would disappear again.

Looking up at his shaven face, the pallor of his skin shocked her. Fatigue had etched deep circles beneath his perfectly normal brown eyes.

"What happened?" she asked, touching his angular jaw. He'd lost weight.

"It's a long story." He smoothed her hair, closing his eyes when his hand contacted the skin of her neck. "But I'm here now."

"I know. I can feel you in here." She pressed her hand to his sternum; their connection had changed timbre. His mind seemed warm now, his body cooler. But the bond remained intact.

"For how long are you back?" It was her best attempt to make the question casual, non-threatening. Anything but desperate.

"As long as you want me to be here." There was lightness about him she'd never sensed before. He no longer radiated anger. The tension around his mouth was gone. In its place was a wry smile.

"Are you … "

"Free?"

"Yes."

His smile crinkled little lines around his eyes. "Oh, yes. I'm completely free now. I'm free to get old and withered, free to lose my mind when the time comes, free to never leave your side."

"How did you—"

"Trade secret." Glancing around furtively, he lifted up his shirt, revealing a jagged scar beneath the center of his ribcage.

Allison gasped.

"Apparently, I was dying to be near you again. You know, I could feel you in my heart as I died."

"I felt you, too. There was pain and then nothing. What does all of this mean?"

He traced her cheek with his index finger. "You have some rules to follow. Now that I'm human, the only way you and your family will remain safe is if you never use your powers to identify one of our kind."

She leaned into his hand, loving the roughness of his palm. "Shouldn't be a problem. I'm better at blocking and filtering these days. If I find another one like you, mum's the word. But what about our connection? I can't stop that."

"I don't think Jerahmeel cares about that anymore. He didn't believe I'd survive the transition back to human."

She traced the red ridge of his scar with shaking fingertips. It was a fresh injury, newly healed. Gooseflesh rose under her touch and she smoothed his shirt back down. "So how was it?"

"How was what?"

"Becoming human."

Grimacing, he squinted up at the Wallowas. "Terrible. Totally worth it."

"Peter, I don't know what to say."

"Say you'll let me stay with you and build a life together. Let me take care of you and help you heal. We'll recuperate together." His voice broke. "I know I've been a killer. I've caused you and your family pain. I have no right to ask for anything."

"You can ask," she whispered, a lump lodged tight in her throat.

He gazed down at her with a calmness and hunger she hadn't seen before. "I need to be with you, Allie. I need *you*. Forever. That's all there is to say."

Tears ran unchecked down her cheeks, and she struggled to catch her breath. He cupped her good elbow and waited as she struggled to compose herself.

After a few minutes, he cleared his throat. "Uh, Allie?"

"Yes?"

"Could you give me some feedback on the part where I said I needed to be with you forever? I'm swinging in the breeze here."

"Oh. *Oh*." She laughed, pulling on his shirt to tug him down so she could kiss him. "Yes, I want you in my life for as long as we live."

Holding her face in his large hands, he rubbed her tears away with the rough pads of his thumbs. "I love you, Allie. I would die for you."

"You already did, Peter. I love you, too." She sank into his embrace until she shivered in the cool air.

"Can I take you back to the house and warm you up?" He kissed her forehead.

She had so much love for him, her heart couldn't expand any further. "Sounds fabulous."

He wrapped an arm around her waist. Peter took Ivy's leash as the happy dog thwacked him in the leg with her tail. He grimaced at the sting.

"Well, I can feel everything now. And it's spectacular!"

Hand in hand, they walked home.

About the Author

Jillian David lives near the end of the Earth with her nut of a husband and two bossy cats. To escape the sometimes-stressful world of the rural physician, she writes while on call and in her free time. She enjoys taking realistic settings and adding a twist of "what if." Running or hiking on local trails often promotes plot development.

A Sneak Peek from Crimson Romance (From *Of Alliance and Rebellion* by Micah Persell)

Somewhere in the deserts of Afghanistan

A moan rent the air, penetrating Max Wright's fitful sleep. The sound rooted its way into his brain, and he buried his head in the crook of his arm. When another moan followed the first, he made his way to wakefulness, prying open gritty eyes.

He blinked once, trying to make sense of the crumbling stone wall inches from his face. Max felt his forehead pucker as he came even more awake. He blinked several more times, but the view never changed, only grew clearer.

Moisture veined the ancient stones with white markings, and the cold night air of the desert penetrated the last of his grogginess. As always happened when Max remembered where he was and why he was here, his hand hovered over his face, fingers trembling, before he brushed them over the raised, ugly flesh that marred him. With the lightest of touches, his pointer finger traced the scar that began at his right temple. A weight settled in his gut as his fingers traveled the path of scar tissue down his ruined eyelid and across his nose to where it ended at the left corner of his jaw.

He licked dry lips. *It was not a dream.*

Another moan, almost a wail, wandered over to where Max lay. With a sigh, he planted one hand on the ratty cot mattress and shoved himself up.

Knowing what he would find when he turned around, he plowed fingers through his matted hair, raking the strands over his right eye. He fought the urge to shake the unruly mop even further over his face. Acting as though it bothered him as much as it did was a show of weakness he could not indulge around the other two prisoners.

Max sucked in a breath and held it until the sting gave him enough courage to face the rest of the cell. Through the dank light filtering in from the cell's only window, Max could see the dark form of Luke huddled over Oliver. Even through the barrier of his hair, Max's ruined right eye zeroed in on the two men with a mental snap that never failed to steal Max's focus. His sliced eye, which was good for practically nothing but this, spoke directly to his mind and informed him that both Luke and Oliver were *good*. It always informed him of this whenever he looked at them, just as it always informed them that their prison wardens—the few that were left—were *evil*.

Useless bits of information. Max gritted his teeth. He already knew his fellow soldiers were good men, and he certainly knew the fuckers who had kept them locked in this cell for nearly nine years were just about as evil as anyone could get.

Max swung his bare feet around and planted them on the stone floor, flinching as his toes encountered frigid rock that had lost the earth's heat soon after sunset. His sudden movement stole Luke's attention, whose gaze collided with Max's. Max again fought the urge to shake his hair over his face. He settled for turning his eye, the worst of his scarring, away, gazing at Luke with his good left eye. Even in the absence of light, Max could see the straining lines at the corners of Luke's mouth.

"Is he still conscious?" Max's sleep-ravaged voice seemed loud in the small cell, bouncing off of the rock that imprisoned them.

Luke's equally dirty nest of red hair brushed his shoulders as he nodded once.

Max hadn't missed the screams while he slept then. He clenched his fists when his hands wanted to tremble. It had been, what, four days since the last time Oliver had—done whatever it was he did every seven days? Max refused to think of it as dying, though that was probably the closest to the truth.

"When's the last time you slept?" Max asked Luke.

Luke sighed before turning his attention back to the twisting form of Oliver.

Max shoved to his feet and shuffled forward. "Come," he said while gesturing to the cot he'd just vacated. "My turn to keep watch."

Luke didn't seem to hear him. He still hovered over Oliver, reaching toward the man once then clenching his hand before allowing it to fall to his knee.

Max glanced at Luke's fingers as they flexed and felt a commiserating bitterness fill his mouth. Neither Max nor Luke could offer Oliver any real comfort. No pats on the shoulder. No holding his hand when the screams started. The lightest touch from either of them only increased Oliver's torture.

"Luke," Max said gently—or at least, as gently as Max could say anything. When Luke jumped like he'd been poked, Max guessed his attempt at *gentle* had far missed the mark. "You can't help him right now. Get some sleep. I'll watch him, I promise."

Luke's light brown eyes, so full of innocence that Max had to remind himself he and Luke were the same age, briefly closed before he got to his feet and walked over to the now-vacant cot, pausing in his stride to pat Max hard on the shoulder, a touch Max tolerated only because he knew it offered Luke comfort.

Max made his way on heavy legs to Oliver's side, feeling Luke's gaze on his back as he settled on the edge of Oliver's cot, making sure that he didn't brush him in the slightest. Luke's stare made the skin stretching over Max's scar burn, even though it was focused on his back, not his face. It wasn't until Luke's breathing evened out and deepened that Max took a breath.

With Luke asleep and relatively safe, Max's responsibilities narrowed down to Oliver. Max focused on Oliver's face—on the scrunched eyes, the thin, grimacing lips almost hidden from view by the unruly beard all three of them sported thanks to several years without access to a razor of any kind.

Those lips parted around a deep moan, and something clenched in Max's chest. "I know, buddy," he whispered to the man, feeling every inch of his uselessness in this situation. "I know."

Oliver's eyelids cracked open. The blue eyes that had charmed many a beautiful woman when they were in the army were now glassy and swimming with pain. "Hurts," he groaned through parched lips. "So bad."

Max cursed on an exhalation of air. "I know," he said again, rage and hopelessness coursing through him.

"The One." Oliver grunted as he tried to shift into a more comfortable position. "I need her."

He was asking for her again. Max's hands clenched on his thighs. That damned woman! Oliver had seen her once. *Once.* Nearly two years ago. He had been ruined ever since.

Quick calculations filtered through Max's head, and he knew Oliver's screaming would start in a few hours. It always did once he began begging for the woman who had left him in such torture with only one look. Tomorrow, Oliver would slip into sleep. Or a coma. Max didn't know what to call it, but whatever it was, Oliver wouldn't wake up from it until he—

Max swallowed thickly. He didn't have to think about that now. He leaned over Oliver, as close as he could without touching, and did the only thing he could do: he talked to the man. Keeping his voice low enough that Luke couldn't hear what he was saying, Max outlined exactly what he would do to their captors once they escaped. It was a list of horrors repeated so often that Max had no problem talking through it without thought.

As always, the lines around Oliver's eyes eased as he took in Max's voice. Whether it was the threats of violence against those who'd wronged them for nine years or the timbre of Max's voice that slightly alleviated Oliver's pain, Max never knew. But this was the only thing that seemed to help, and so Max would recite his plan for revenge until he went hoarse if necessary.

The list was long and took Max several hours to get through. He paused only once: when one of the handful of guards who remained in the prison tossed a dried lump of bread and discolored bladder of water through the bars. As soon as the guard shuffled away, Max continued. Rage twisted his words as Oliver's hands clenched the mattress beneath him, his back bowing, his head snapping back. The first scream of what would be many was wrenched from the man's chest, echoing around the cell loudly.

Luke sat up with a snort, jerked from sleep. He raced over to Oliver's cot as Max rose to unsteady feet. "Oliver," Luke said on a breath. "You're okay." Luke sat down where Max had been moments before. "You're okay, man, you're okay."

Max ran his tongue along his teeth and took a step back before he could strangle Luke. Oliver was most definitely *not* okay, and all three of them knew it.

Max spun around, seeing nothing but red as another scream broke from Oliver's now thrashing body. "*Fuck!*" Max bellowed. His fist snapped out before he could stop it, colliding with the stone wall hard enough that his hand broke.

Luke jumped, but didn't glance his way as Max gave a cursory glance at the cracked skin of his knuckles while it began to mend. The sight of his body supernaturally healing due to what their captors had done to him only enraged him more. He clenched his fists at his sides and let the blood from his hand drip to the floor unchecked.

As Luke leaned over Oliver, whispered prayers tumbling from his mouth, Max paced back and forth, mentally repeating his diatribe of promised revenge until Oliver's screams grew loud enough to block out even that. To purchase this ebook and learn more about the author, *click here.*

In the mood for more Crimson Romance?
Check out *An Angel Fallen by Holley Trent* at *CrimsonRomance.com*.

Printed in the United States
By Bookmasters